Whispering Rooms

Whispering Rooms

Genki Kawamura and
Marie Kondo

Translated by Cathy Hirano

Illustrations by Yosuke Omomo

First published in 2022 in Japan by Chuokoron-Shinsa
First published in the UK in 2026 by LEAP
An imprint of Bonnier Books UK
5th Floor, HYLO, 105 Bunhill Row,
London, EC1Y 8LZ

Copyright © Genki Kawamura, Inc. and KonMari Media, Inc. 2026
English translation copyright © Cathy Hirano
Illustration copyright © Yosuke Omomo

All rights reserved.

No part of this publication may be reproduced, stored or transmitted in any form or by any means, electronic, mechanical, photocopying or otherwise, without the prior written permission of the publisher.

The right of Genki Kawamura and Marie Kondo to be identified as Authors of this work has been asserted by them in accordance with the Copyright, Designs and Patents Act, 1988.

A CIP catalogue record for this book is available from the British Library.

Paperback ISBN: 9781806170586

Also available as an ebook and an audiobook

1 3 5 7 9 10 8 6 4 2

Design and Typeset by Envy Design Ltd
Printed and bound by CPI (UK) Ltd, Croydon CR0 4YY

Every reasonable effort has been made to trace copyright holders of material reproduced in this book, but if any have been inadvertently overlooked the publishers would be glad to hear from them.

The authorised representative in the EEA is
Bonnier Books UK (Ireland) Limited.
Registered office address: Block B, The Crescent Building
Northwood, Santry
Dublin 9, D09 C6X8, Ireland
compliance@bonnierbooks.ie

www.bonnierbooks.co.uk

Contents

Prologue		1
Room 1	The Whispering Wardrobe	3
Room 2	The Singing Study	33
Room 3	The Bickering Kitchen	61
Room 4	The Silent Childhood Bedroom	89
Room 5	The Chatty Little Box	115

Room 6 The Hoarder's Noisy Trash	141
Room 7 Storytelling Photo Albums	169
Epilogue	199
Miko's Tidying Tips	201

Prologue

I've got a secret I can't tell anyone.

I can hear things talk.

Clothes, shoes, books, furniture – when I walk into a room, they all talk to me.

My job is helping people to tidy up their homes.

And here beside me is my tidying buddy: a chatty little box.

I suppose this must sound odd.

Maybe you're wondering how tidying could be a job.

Or how someone can hear things talk.

Or what I mean when I say that my buddy is a box. But all these things are true.

I've tidied over a thousand homes. And each room

in those homes overflowed with the memories and thoughts of the people who lived there and of the chatty things they owned.

Let me share with you a few of those stories.

Stories about some of the unusual rooms I've encountered.

ROOM 1
The Whispering Wardrobe

Mayuko Aizawa (age 49)

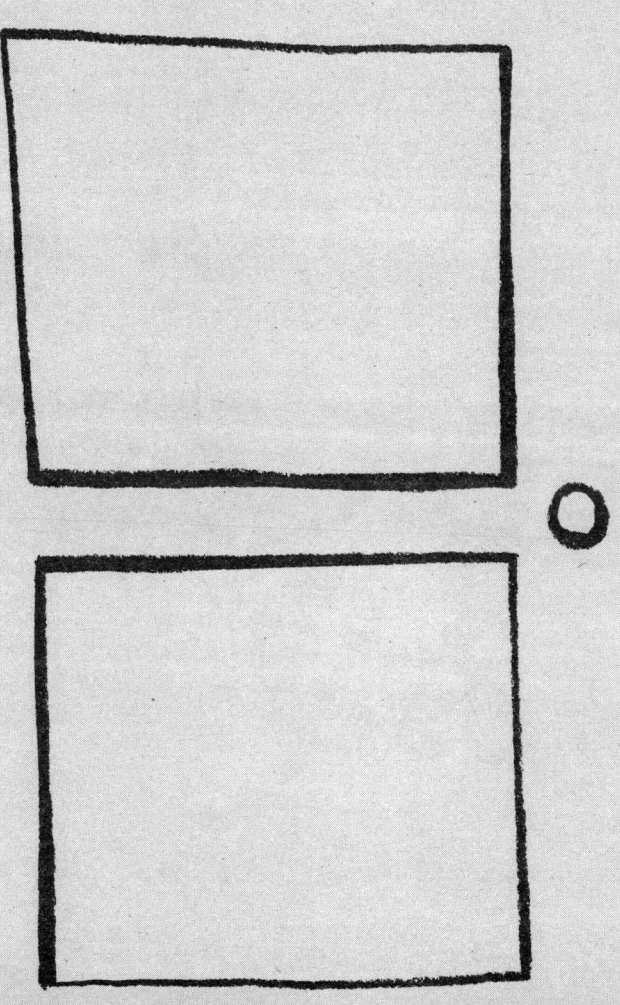

As I opened the door and stepped into the room, I was greeted by smells reminiscent of a crowded rummage sale – a mix of perfume, sanitiser spray and ingrained sweat. The room had once been a child's room, but now cast-off clothes lay strewn across the floor like flotsam washed up on a beach.

I heard voices. Female voices. Hundreds of them. The clothes had all started talking at once.

Oh dear, is another new outfit going to join us?
Give me a break.
When will it be my turn to be worn?
Who's that lady?

Those that still knew they were clothes could be heard more clearly, but the voices of the 'used-to-be-clothes' strewn in heaps about the room sounded more like screams than words.

It's all right, I said inwardly. *I'm here to help.*

I tightened the red neckerchief I wore with my white dress, then placed my palms together in front of my chest and bowed deeply.

A voice came from behind me. 'I bet you were shocked by the mess.'

I turned to see Mayuko Aizawa, my client. Her hands gripped the hem of her apron, which she wore over a frilly dress.

'No, not at all,' I said. 'People usually hire me when they've got to the point that they don't know what to do. Just thinking about how to tidy this up gives me a thrill.' I smiled, but her eyes were fixed on my dress.

'You'll get that nice white dress dirty if you tidy in it.'

'For me, tidying is like a sacred festival, so I want to look my best,' I reassured her. 'And besides, you're the one who will do the actual tidying. I'm just here to help.'

I took a box from my shoulder bag and walked further into her room, taking care not to step on any of the clothes. Piles of underwear that hadn't been folded littered the floor, dresses and coats were packed into the built-in wardrobe like sushi in a box, and T-shirts oozed from the dresser in the corner like filling in a double-decker hamburger.

The Whispering Wardrobe

As I walked around, anxious whispers spread through the room – the voices of clothes which only I could hear.

What's going on?

I've got a bad feeling about this.

And like I said, who is she?

'I couldn't figure out where to start,' Mayuko said as she followed timidly behind me. She ran a hand nervously along her neck where wrinkles were starting to show. 'Do you think it's really possible to tidy this up?'

'Don't worry. I'm sure you can do it.' I smiled again.

The box, which I had tucked under my arm, cracked open his lid and said, *There you go again, Miko. How can you say that so breezily when you know how much work it's going to be? You're always too optimistic.*

'It'll be fine, you'll see,' I told him. This cheeky box with white and blue stripes is my tidying buddy. I call him Hako, which means 'box' in Japanese. He has been coming with me to my clients' houses for the last four years or so, and as Miko & Hako, we make a pretty good team. How did I end up working with a box? Well, one of these days, I'll tell you that story too, but right now it's time to get to work!

I gave Mayuko her first mission. 'Please take out all your clothes,' I said.

Her eyes grew round. 'All of them?'

'Yes, all of them. And not just the ones in here. Bring everything you've got from every room and pile them in one place.'

The clothes began to clamour.

I was having such a nice deep sleep! How could you disturb me?

What's she up to?

I bet she's going to throw us all away!

Ignoring their voices, I began helping Mayuko as she removed the clothes from her wardrobe. Next, we tackled the dresser, emptying it of all the T-shirts, socks, hats, etc. Thirty minutes later there was a multicoloured mountain in the middle of the room.

'Do you have any other clothes or is this everything?' I asked.

'I think that's all.'

'You'll have to let go of any other clothes that turn up after this, so please make sure.'

'Um ... wait a moment. There might be a jacket hanging over the back of a chair in the dining room.

Oh, and maybe something on the wall of my bedroom.'

She dashed out and quickly returned with a jacket and a coat. These two made it safely onto the pile of clothes.

'Hold on a sec,' she said. 'There's some stuff in the washing machine too.'

'Clothes in the wash are okay,' I said.

'That's a relief,' she sighed.

But something didn't seem quite right. Although she'd told me she lived in this apartment with her husband, I hadn't seen any sign of him. 'Is your husband going to join us?' I asked.

'He's not interested in tidying,' she said. 'I don't think he has any idea what's here or even what kind of clothes I wear.'

Oh-oh. What's all this? Don't they get along? hissed Box, glancing at Mayuko's forlorn expression.

'Quiet,' I whispered, shutting his mouth, or rather his lid, firmly.

Mayuko's eyes were fixed on the pile in the middle of the room. 'So here are all my clothes, but ... what should I do next?'

I pulled back the curtains, which had been shut tight,

and opened the window, letting in a flood of sunlight and the cool autumn breeze. Little birds darted across the mackerel sky. I turned to Mayuko, who was squinting up at the birds. 'Start by thinking about your ideal lifestyle,' I said, 'the kind of life you'd like to lead.'

'My ideal lifestyle …'

'Visualise concretely how you want to spend your time in this space.'

'I have no idea. I've never thought about it,' she murmured. 'Our kids have grown up now, so I just thought I'd live quietly with my husband. It never occurred to me there could be any other way. I can't even begin to imagine.' She paused and remained silent for a while.

I held her gaze and said, 'You don't have to come up with an answer right away. Just keep one thing in mind.

The Whispering Wardrobe

You should keep things and discard things for the same reason: because that's what makes you happy. That's the most important point in tidying up.'

'Because it makes me happy,' she repeated, as if mulling this over. Although she looked puzzled, I could see that she was searching for her own answers.

I knelt down in front of the pile of clothes. 'From here, you will choose what you want to keep and what you want to let go.'

'How?'

'By asking yourself whether or not it sparks joy.'

'Joy? But how will I know?'

'Simple. By touching them. You'll know if something gives you joy when you hold it in your hands.'

She looked a little anxious. Maybe she'd been expecting a more logical approach to tidying.

See. Just like I keep telling you, Hako grumbled from his hiding place under my arm. *Now she thinks you're weird too.*

'Shush!' I whispered as I pulled him out.

You don't seem to get it, but your approach seems kind of occult. I mean like seriously unscientific. No wonder people get suspicious.

'Stop that!' I said under my breath.

'Is something wrong?' Mayuko was looking at the box in my hands.

I whipped it behind my back and shook my head. 'No. Nothing.' She'd only think I was weirder if I told her I was talking to a box.

Clients often look bewildered when I tell them to choose what to keep based on whether it sparks joy. Some probably wonder if I'm a con artist. Even so, I always hope people will give it a try, at least once. Our bodies respond differently to each physical object we come in contact with. If we gather every item that falls into the same category in one spot, pick them up one at a time and ask whether it sparks joy, once we're done, we'll find we're left with only the things we really need.

Instead of choosing what to throw away, we should choose what to keep. That's the first step of tidying up:

selecting only those things we feel will bring us joy and letting go of all the rest.

'But I haven't a clue where to start,' Mayuko said.

I pointed to a pair of shorts which would be too cold for fall. 'I recommend starting with off-season clothes,' I said.

'Why?' Mayuko asked, picking up a thin blouse.

'If you start with clothes you might wear right now, your joy sensor can't function objectively. You'll start thinking, "I just wore this yesterday", or worry that you won't have anything left to wear.'

'I guess that makes sense.'

'Also, the selection criterion for off-season clothes is clear. Just ask yourself if you're eager to wear it when it comes back in season. As for those things you decide not to keep, remember to thank them for all their hard work before setting them aside. Why don't you give it a try? Otherwise, you'll never know if it really works or not!'

Maybe my little pep talk encouraged her. She reached tentatively towards the pile.

Try me on. You'll look much younger, shouted a short skirt.

I'll make you look pretty, exclaimed a blouse with a ribbon.

I can make you look slimmer, declared a dress with panels.

They're all so full of themselves, aren't they? complained Hako.

'Don't say that,' I muttered.

You'll look younger, prettier, slimmer. Although Mayuko couldn't hear them, judging from what her clothes were saying, they all should have been bringing her joy. The stream of sweet words was unceasing, yet there wasn't even a hint of joy in Mayuko's expression as she held each one. She paused, staring at the dress clutched in her hands.

'How about that one? Does it spark joy?' I asked.

'I've ... never worn it,' Mayuko murmured without answering my question.

I turned the dress over. Sure enough, the price tag was still on. 'Whether you've worn it or not, if it doesn't spark joy, let it go.'

'But that's such a waste!'

'Even though you'd forgotten that you bought it?'

While helping people tidy, I often find clothes with the price tags still on or underwear still in the package. Although these articles are in their own home where they should feel comfortable, they look stiff and ill at ease. Clothes that haven't graduated from being 'store items' will never be worn. Their owners may be convinced

they'll wear them 'someday', but months and years inevitably pass without that ever happening. To avoid this, I recommend taking them out of their packages and removing the tags as soon as you get home from the shop. The ritual of severing the umbilical cord connecting apparel to the store is essential if they are to leave behind their life as 'shop items' and begin life as members of their owner's home.

I waded through a thicket of dresses and stumbled into a dense clump of shirts and blouses. Looking closely, I saw two that were exactly the same cut but different colours: one light blue and the other pink.

'Mayuko,' I said. 'Why do you have two of these?'

'I really liked the design so I bought the same shirt in a different colour.' She reached out and took one in each hand.

The voice of the blue shirt sounded in my ears. *Why don't you do some work for a change?*

What're you talking about? retorted the pink shirt. *Imagine yourself stuck at home all day like me, just waiting.*

It's your own fault! You're not trying hard enough! If you want to be worn, you should pretty yourself up.

Don't talk down to me! I'm not like you!

Mayuko, oblivious to their bickering, pondered the two shirts for a while, then decided to keep the blue one.

Goodbye then!

And good riddance!

Hako opened his lid timidly to take a peek. *Ooh! Sibling spats are gruesome!*

'But considering the circumstances, I can understand how they feel,' I said.

True. Looks like the blue one got worn a lot more than the pink. The blue one looks radiant because she was kept in good condition, while the pink one is still stuck in the package she came in.

I frequently come across this kind of sibling rivalry when I'm tidying clothes. Although many people buy shirts or trousers of the same cut in different colours, in most cases, they end up wearing only one of the pair. I feel sorry for the one that is never worn. Despite being so similar, it's clear their sibling is the favourite.

Interestingly, this same trend occurs even when people buy identical garments of the exact same cut and colour. For some reason, one of the two is always chosen while the other is not. Squabbles between such identical twins can be spectacularly spiteful.

'This doesn't spark joy either ... even though I loved it when I bought it.' Mayuko was looking regretfully at a jacket she'd only worn a few times. It was a pink tweed with shiny black buttons. Despite having been one of her favourites, it had been stored at the bottom of a box. When clothes are piled in a box, the ones on the bottom have even less chance of being worn. Many times, clothes that people love when they first buy them end up forgotten in a pile once they stop sparking joy.

All I wanted was to be loved, the jacket said huskily.

Something prompted me to check the pockets. I slipped my hand in one and pulled out a ticket stub for a movie. A love story that had been a huge hit five years ago. It was hard to believe that creaseless stub was five years old.

'I went with my husband,' Mayuko whispered, her eyes fixed on the ticket stub in my hand. 'We still went out for dinner and to the movies then. These days, we don't do that kind of thing ...'

I could think of nothing to say. Sometimes, tidying up confronts us with a cruel reality.

Just as I thought. This couple's in trouble, huh, Hako commented.

'It's none of your business,' I hissed and shut his mouth (or rather his lid).

Mayuko hugged the jacket to her chest. 'This doesn't spark joy anymore. It seems to be the only thing that still treasures those memories.'

'I get the feeling it wants you to let it go, too,' I said gently. 'I think it wants to go out and see the world.'

Why did I buy this? Why did I stop wearing it? Pondering such questions when we part with something is far from a waste of time. When we find it hard to let a particular garment go, it's important to reflect on its true purpose in our lives. Often, we'll see that its role was to teach us what doesn't suit us. The moment we realise this, the garment has fulfilled its mission. We can thank it for the thrill it gave us when we bought it and for teaching us what doesn't look good on us. Then we can let it go, as if sending off its spirit, confident that it will return to us in another form.

For the next two hours, Mayuko sorted her clothes into those that sparked joy and those that didn't. When she finished, the volume of the first category was much less than that of the second. Frankly, even I was surprised at how few clothes she'd chosen to keep.

'I thought these were all my favourites,' she said as she stroked the clothes she had decided to discard. 'But I don't wear any of them anymore. Even though they should have brought me joy. I wonder why.'

I clapped my hands to dispel the gloom and said brightly, 'Now that you've chosen what to keep, it's time to store them.' I whispered to Hako, 'It's your turn.'

All right, he said in a slightly bored voice. He slipped

The Whispering Wardrobe

out of Mayuko's line of sight and opened his mouth wide. Like a set of Russian nesting dolls, one box popped out after another, each one a little smaller in size than the one before it.

I use boxes for storing all kinds of things and would go so far as to claim that they're the key to perfect storage. On Hako's cue, all the boxes opened their mouths – or rather, lids – wide and stood at the ready. Time to start!

But Mayuko didn't move. 'I don't know where to store what,' she said with a frown.

She seemed overwhelmed by all the storage options staring her in the face – the wardrobe, the chest of drawers, clothes boxes, cardboard boxes ...

She can't make up her mind! No wonder she ends up with so much stuff! Hako complained, his lid flapping. I clamped his lid shut and smiled at Mayuko.

'My tidying method can be summed up in just two steps,' I said.

'Just two?'

'Yes. Deciding what to let go of and deciding where the things you've chosen to keep belong. Just those two things.'

'Deciding where they belong.'

'Identify the things that bring you joy, then decide where you want to store them. These two simple practices will keep you from reverting to clutter.'

'But how should I decide what goes where?' Mayuko's gaze shifted to the pile of clothes. They immediately began clamouring for attention.

A pleated skirt stretched, exclaiming, *I've been squeezed into a storage box for so long, I want to be hung so I can move freely.*

A tailored jacket declared, *I absolutely refuse to be folded. Be sure to choose a good-quality hanger, too! My dignity depends upon it!*

With their words echoing in my mind, I suggested,

'Let's hang up any clothes that look like they'd be happier that way.'

'Happier?'

Ha. There you go again, Miko, said Hako. *Saying weird stuff. She's going to think you're nuts.*

Ignoring him, I continued. 'For example, things like light, frilly skirts that enjoy dancing on the breeze or jackets that would object to being folded. Let's try hanging them.'

'Miko, you talk as if you can hear what those clothes are saying,' said Mayuko.

That's because she can, you know, muttered Hako and stuck out his tongue, which was actually a pink ribbon.

To demonstrate, I picked a long coat out of the pile and put it on a hanger, then together, we did the same with many other items she'd decided to keep. 'Now that you've decided which clothes should be hung up, let's hang everything rising to the right,' I said.

'Rising to the right?'

'Clothes that are longer, heavier material and darker colours go on the left and then transition to shorter, lighter materials and brighter colours to the right. As for categories, start with coats on the left, then dresses, jackets, slacks, skirts and blouses. Clothes feel safer and more secure when they're stored by category.'

'Safe and secure? You say some interesting things.' Mayuko smiled.

'But don't you think my rule is kind of neat?' After a bit of reordering, I drew a line in the air rising to the right, and Mayuko looked at the clothes in her wardrobe which were now arranged from left to right.

'Yes, actually. They do look happy.'

'Next, we'll move on to folding. You can store two or three times as much in the same space just by folding your clothes.'

'It makes that much difference?'

'Yes. It draws on the principles of Japanese origami.'

'Is there some special technique or something?' She tilted her head to one side as she looked down at the wool sweater in her hands.

I stroked a T-shirt that lay in front of me. 'The trick is to communicate with your clothes. Let them know through the touch of your hand that you love them. In your mind, say, "Thank you for protecting me and for keeping me warm." This energises your clothes and makes them last longer.'

'I see. Maybe that's why we were always told as kids to treat things with care.'

Mayuko and I sat on the floor and folded T-shirts and sweaters into smooth rectangles. Meanwhile, Hako kept up a steady stream of instructions, making sure his companions were standing by when we needed them.

Suddenly I heard a strangled gasp.

Ugh, that's too tight.

Ach, I'm choking.

Turning to look, I saw Mayuko tying her stockings into bundles and folding the tops of her socks over each pair to make balls. 'Mayuko, they look very uncomfortable!' I exclaimed without thinking.

'What?'

'Your stockings. Please don't tie them in knots, or ball your socks either. It's better to fold them instead.' I undid a knotted pair of stockings and showed her how to neatly fold them. 'It's better to pack folded stockings together in a small box so that they hold the folds easily. That way they don't hog space either, which makes for peaceful storage.'

'Er, whose is this?'

'... Um, mine.'

'You don't wear it anymore ... do you?'

'No. Not anymore.'

We had finished storing almost all the clothes. Alone on the floor of the almost empty room lay a sailor suit uniform. It had been stored in a large box hidden away in the back of the wardrobe. Mayuko had left that box to the very end before dragging it out.

'So why can't I bring myself to throw it away?' She hung her head as if embarrassed.

Suddenly, I heard laughter. A girl's voice. I stroked the uniform. An image rose into my mind. Mayuko as a teenager, sitting on the back of a bike. A tall young man in a black high school uniform with a straight-collared jacket and brass buttons was pedalling. Mayuko's arms were wrapped around his waist and her face was beaming as they cycled along the edge of a lake.

Miko, did you see something? His work finished, Hako waddled closer with his lid ajar.

'Uh-huh.' Sometimes I see the memories of the owner when I touch a piece of clothing.

What?

The Whispering Wardrobe

'Mayuko, when she was in senior high.'

Mayuko sat in the middle of her room, hugging the sailor uniform to her chest. 'This is my senior high school uniform,' she said quietly. 'It was the first thing my friends ever said looked good on me. I was ecstatic because I'd never had confidence in the clothes I wore. Maybe it was thanks to that, but a guy I thought was cool told me he liked me and we began dating. We stayed together all through senior high and university.'

'What a lovely story,' I said, my voice bright with excitement. It seemed like a romance from a girl's manga.

'We got married, too,' she continued. 'But now ...'

But now that same guy didn't know what was here,

showed no interest in what she wore, no longer went to the movies with her, and didn't care to participate in tidying up.

'Mayuko, why don't you try it on?'

'What?'

'The uniform.'

Her eyes grew round.

Miko, are you crazy? Hako gaped at me.

'All right. I will.' Even I was surprised by Mayuko's courageous response. She took off her apron and began changing into the uniform.

You've got to be kidding. Hako shut his lid as though trying to cover his eyes.

When Mayuko had finished changing, I handed her a mirror. She looked into it hesitantly. The reflection was undoubtedly that of a middle-aged woman dressed in a high school uniform. She'd gained weight since she'd been a student, and fine wrinkles were visible on her neck and cheeks. Her shoulders began to shake, and she buried her face in her hands.

See what you've done! Hako said crossly, but I kept my eyes fixed on Mayuko. I was sure there was a meaning in this.

Suddenly, she began to laugh. Her laughter grew louder, shaking her whole body. 'Look at that old lady wearing a high school uniform!'

Hako cast me an anxious glance. *Is she okay? Has she lost her mind?*

'Don't worry,' I told him.

After laughing for some time, Mayuko wiped the tears from her eyes and said, 'I'm going to throw this uniform away. And I'm going to say goodbye to my husband, too.' Her smile was radiant and her face, flushed. 'I've finally made up my mind. I feel like this uniform is telling me it's okay to forget.'

I just looked at her without saying anything. She took off the uniform and changed into a pair of slacks and a blouse with a simple, elegant silhouette which she picked from the clothes that brought her joy.

'The two sons I had after we married are all grown up. They've graduated from university and started working. Once I sent them off into the world and it was just my husband and me, I realised something: we're not interested in each other anymore.'

She placed the uniform tenderly on the pile she had decided to part with. 'For ages, I haven't been able to accept that in myself. I wanted to be the way I was when I was young, so I kept choosing clothes that would make me look younger or that used to look good on me. Which is why I don't have anything that suits me now. Despite having all these clothes, none of them bring me joy and I've got nothing to wear.'

I've always thought that tidying up means confronting your feelings. Living for so long with clothes she didn't like had made it hard for Mayuko to know what suited her or what she really loved. Through tidying, people come face to face with problems they've been trying to ignore, and are forced to resolve them, like it or not. That's actually the first step to finding real happiness.

'I've finally realised why I asked you to help me tidy up, Miko,' said Mayuko. 'I want to live surrounded only by things I love. I want to know what I need in my life, and what I don't. It's like you were saying. I think I wanted to tidy up my past so I could be happy in the present. I'm grateful to you, Miko. So please don't cry.'

I was startled to find that tears were flowing down my cheeks. I didn't even know why I was crying.

'Mayuko,' I said. There was so much I wanted to tell her, but I couldn't find my voice. For once, chatty little

Hako also remained silent, as if keeping me company. Mayuko cast her eyes around the tidy room. It was filled with sunshine. A refreshing breeze blew through the window, and the clothes hanging in her wardrobe swayed as if with delight.

I heard the sailor uniform say, *You'll find clothes just right for you. I know you will.*

'I wonder what I should do next. I can't make tidying my profession like you, but I am good at baking bread. Recently, I started working part-time at a local bakery, and I love it. When I was a kid, I used to dream of opening my own bakery.'

The sun fell on her, accentuating the flattering cut of the clothes she had chosen. She had the strength and beauty of a woman who has lived her life well.

'What a lovely dream. When you open your bakery, I'll be sure to go.'

'Thank you. You'll be the first person I invite.' She smiled, her face lighting up with the satisfaction of someone who has set everything in order.

ROOM 2
The Singing Study

Kunio Midorikawa (age 60)

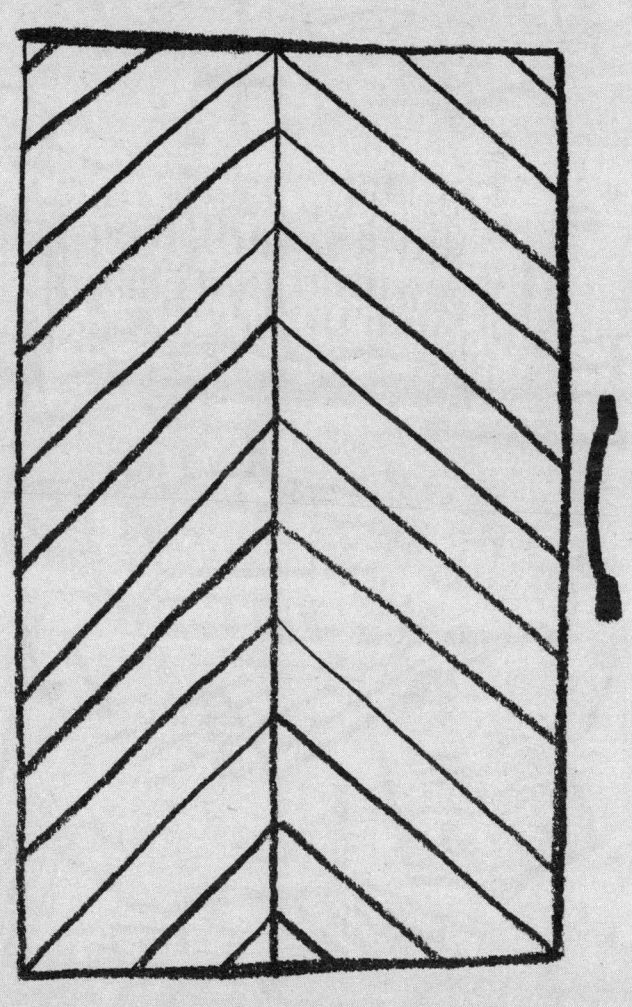

I climbed the stairs to the second floor and opened the door at the top. Music washed over me in waves. The books were singing.

Built-in bookcases covered three walls of the room from floor to ceiling, and these were tightly packed with books of every size stacked vertically, horizontally and even diagonally, like pieces in an intricate jigsaw puzzle. The overflow lay in piles not only on the desk but also on the floor. All the books sang lustily, each pursuing its own melody.

Nestled in the crook of my arm, Hako screwed up his face. *That's some crazy choir, isn't it?*

'Shhh. Don't say that. I'm sure if we just listen ...' I closed my eyes and cocked my ears.

The books I encounter when tidying up almost always sing. A light bossa nova rises from books on handicrafts or gardening, while manga lean towards lively music like pop songs, rock, punk or techno. Picture books sound like children's songs, and poetry anthologies often sound like cabaret or sometimes even rap. If I walk into a store where the books are humming Baroque music, I know the shelves are likely to be full of philosophy or academic works.

A person's life is condensed in their bookshelves. The type of books they have determines the kind of music a room emits, and I can usually tell what my client is like just by listening. But not today. The songs reverberating in this room created such a cacophony, I couldn't grasp a thing.

I stood so long with my eyes closed that Hako finally nudged me (or, more accurately, bumped me with the corner of his lid). *Well, what do you think?* he asked.

'I don't get any of it!'

Just as I thought. An abominable band.

'Not a crazy choir?'

Same thing, Hako said cockily sticking out his pink-ribbon tongue.

'There's no need to tidy this room,' said a deep voice behind me. I turned and saw my client, Kunio Midorikawa, peeking into the room from the doorway.

The Singing Study

I guessed he'd finished tidying his clothes and had come upstairs to find me. His grey hair was slicked back, and his round face was adorned with tortoiseshell glasses. Although he was in his own home, he wore a tweed jacket, which gave him the impression of being a meticulous kind of person.

'What do you mean?' My voice came out in a squeak. How could he say there was no need to tidy this room when it was such a mess?

'Well, they're books, you know. Not much you can do about them, is there?' he said.

'But it's quite cluttered.'

'I know. Still, I don't see how we can tidy them. My wife keeps nagging me to do it, but I'm just not comfortable unless I'm surrounded by books. I can't get any inspiration. Besides, I'm not the type to enjoy a minimalist lifestyle.' His eyes slithered away from the books as he spoke.

Hey! Over here! shouted a rock-and-roller voice. *Time to read me, man. Y'got that?*

This pronouncement was overlapped by a plaintive folk song. *Long ago and far away, you read me every single day!*

A high soprano voice broke into a solo. *While I, alas, have never been opened, let alone read.*

These individual melody tracks were punctuated by a rapper's beat. *Consider yourself lucky to be on a shelf! Here on the floor, I need some help. Stuck at the bottom of a pile unread. Who knows how long? Might as well be dead.*

All these clamouring voices were directed at Mr Midorikawa where he stood uneasily on the threshold. And of course, none of them reached his ears.

Geez. Now they've become an obstreperous opera!

'Hold your tongue, Hako!' I whispered fiercely, pressing his lid down.

Mr Midorikawa raised his eyebrows. 'What did you say?'

'Nothing!' I said in a singsong voice, influenced by the chorus of books. He was going to think my behaviour very suspicious. This wasn't a musical in which characters suddenly burst into song. Pulling myself together, I shifted my gaze to the piles of books.

'So, if you don't mind, Miko,' Mr Midorikawa continued, 'please go tidy somewhere else.' He ran his eyes around the room, then turned his back on it abruptly.

'Mr Midorikawa,' I said.

'Yes?' he responded without turning to look.

'As I mentioned at the beginning, it's you, not me, who does the tidying.'

'Oh, that's right. Pardon me.'

'If you leave your study like this, you'll never know what's really important to you.'

When I had arrived in the morning, Mr Midorikawa had met me at the door. He explained with a sheepish look that his wife told him she'd had enough of his mess and that he'd better get his act together and tidy up. 'But I can't help it,' he'd said. 'Things just seem to pile up with each passing year.'

'You know what you have the most of?' I said now. He paused and turned to look at me. 'Books.' I ran my index finger along the cover of one of the books lying on his desk and showed it to him. The tip was covered in dust.

Sheesh, Hako chuckled, opening his lid a crack. *You're just like a nasty mother-in-law.*

Refusing to take the bait, I continued. 'There's an order to tidying up. We start with clothes, then move on to books and papers, then things we use in daily life and miscellaneous items, finishing off with things

of sentimental value. This order is important, so please don't jump to some other category first.'

'But I can't possibly do anything about my books.'

'You did a great job with clothes just now, didn't you? It's the same process.'

Mr Midorikawa had finished sorting his clothes in less than two hours that morning. He didn't have many clothes to start with and was able to choose those that sparked joy and those that didn't very quickly.

'I don't have any fashion sense, so I'm not particularly attached to clothes,' he said meekly. 'But when it comes to books, I'm not confident I could get rid of any.'

'Why?'

'Well, I'll be retiring soon, you see, after working many years as a newspaper reporter in charge of the cultural section.'

'So that's why you have such a wide selection of books. You're a real bookworm.'

'I'm not sure I deserve the title of bookworm. I think of myself more as a random reader. I just find it really difficult to let go of books, whether they're gifts or ones I bought myself, and whether I've read them or not. That's why my study looks like this. It's pathetic, really.'

I've encountered a lot of bookshelves in my work and have come to see books as manifestations of their owner's longings. Some convey dread; the fear of things we shouldn't eat, shouldn't buy, or shouldn't believe. Others represent the owner's wishes about the kind of person they want to be or things they want to try. Mr Midorikawa's study was essentially a forest of dreams and aspirations – which made getting rid of anything a challenge.

'There's nothing wrong with having lots of books,' I told him. 'As long as you can cherish them all. Even if you decide not to discard a single book, that's totally fine. So, let's start by taking them off the shelves. If you leave your study like this, it's nothing but a book graveyard.' I deliberately chose this harsh expression. Sorting his books would be a formidable task, but I knew that once it was done, the momentum gained would propel him quickly through the rest of the tidying process.

'A graveyard ...' Robbed of speech, Mr Midorikawa peered through the door into the study. After gazing at the books for a while, he seemed to make up his mind and stepped inside.

I bowed and thanked him for agreeing to cooperate.

'No, no, thank you,' he said, bobbing his head in return. 'Sorry to behave like a spoiled brat.' I had thought he was a nervous person but now realised he was probably just shy and a little timid. I gave him an encouraging smile, then tightened my red neckerchief to psych myself up.

'Please put all the books on the floor, just like we did for clothes.'

Mr Midorikawa began working on a bookcase at the far end of the room. 'The volume's overwhelming, isn't it?' he murmured. Dust danced in the air, sparkling in the light of the small lamp on his desk. 'But why do it this way when it's so time-consuming?' he asked, gripping a stack of thick catalogues of artists like Paul Cézanne and Amedeo Modigliani. 'After all, we'll just be putting most of them back on the shelves anyway.'

'There are two reasons why it's better to remove all your books from the shelves. One is to get an accurate grasp of the sheer volume of what you have. The other is to wake them up.'

'Wake them up?'

Oh-oh, Hako said in an exasperated tone. *There you*

go, trotting out that spiritual stuff again, Miko. People always think you're nuts. You'd better quit doing that.

I ignored him and ploughed on. 'If they're left inactive too long, books doze off. And not just books, but also clothes and other things. It's as if they've become invisible or disappeared from existence. Many of them only remember they exist when someone picks them up. Even you had almost completely forgotten what books were in this room, right?'

'Yes, that's true,' Mr Midorikawa said. He stared at an introductory book on Japanese drumming in his hands. 'I wonder when I bought this,' he murmured, shaking his head.

'If you don't take them off the shelves and sort them now, we'll have to come back again once we finish all the other rooms. That's why you shouldn't skip this step. You should move the books piled on the floor, too, even if it's just to push them to a slightly different spot or restack them. It will make it much easier to choose.'

Mr Midorikawa timidly unstacked and then restacked a pile of philosophical works on the floor – things like *Essais* by Michel de Montaigne and *Pensées* by Blaise Pascal – followed by a pile of manga, including *Akira* by

The Singing Study

Katsuhiro Otomo and *Dororo* by Osamu Tezuka. Books that had been packed into the bookshelves and stacked on the desk and chair now covered the entire floor. Within less than an hour, the floor of the study had been transformed into a cityscape of book high-rises.

Mr Midorikawa made his way gingerly between the rows of skyscrapers. 'Now what do we do?' he asked with a note of panic in his voice.

'The same thing we do for every other category. Touch each one and, if it sparks joy, keep it. If it doesn't, let it go.'

As he listened to my words, Mr Midorikawa stared at the piles of books at his feet. A host of introductory handbooks on gardening, ballroom dancing, history exams, pottery, painting, etc. chimed in, each with its own distinctive voice.

Hello! How are you? an English conversation book called out brightly.

Namu Amida Butsu, chanted a sutra-tracing book.

What a wonderful world, sang a beginner's jazz book.

Hako clutched his head. *Whoa! Is he trying to start a correspondence school or something?*

Mr Midorikawa crouched down and picked up a

book. I knelt down across from him and peered into his face. 'What do you think? Does it spark joy?'

'Hmm. I'm not sure. Maybe it will soon.'

'Soon?'

'I'll be retiring soon. I think I'll read it once I've retired.'

'But does it bring you joy now?'

'I'm not sure.'

'If it's a book you're about to read soon, it should already be bringing you joy *now*.'

'But ... it would be a waste to throw it away if I haven't even read it.'

'Isn't it more of a waste to spend your time thinking you might read it someday or feeling guilty because you ought to read it?'

The Singing Study

'Maybe you're right.' Mr Midorikawa stroked the introductory books with a forlorn look.

I often run into mountains of 'how to' books when tidying up. Almost none of them have been properly read. All my clients say they plan to read them 'someday'. But 'someday' never comes.

As Mr Midorikawa regretfully placed the book on the discard pile, I said, 'I think the things in our lives have different roles. The role of some books is to be read only partway through. There's always meaning in the books that come to you. Even if you decide to let them go, what they've given you will come back to serve you in some way.'

'It's true that some books inspire absolutely nothing when I touch them. Even though I read them with so much interest,' he murmured. He was holding a business book that had been a big hit about five years ago. It was singing opera with great pride and dignity. But it was off-key and seemed ill at ease.

When tidying, I've noticed that bestsellers like the one in his hand seem to have a season in which they are all discarded. The joy wears off as if everyone is waking from the same dream simultaneously, and the books graduate from everyone's bookshelves at once. It's as if people unconsciously share some kind of sixth sense.

'I'd like to take my time with this and think about it,' Mr Midorikawa said. He knelt down among the book skyscrapers, as if shifting into gear. 'Miko, why don't you go down to the living room and have some tea?'

'Thank you. I'll take you up on that and have a little break.' I bowed, left the study and headed downstairs.

Mr Midorikawa's wife greeted me as I entered the living room. She brought me some green tea and ohagi:

balls of sticky rice coated in adzuki bean paste.

'How's it going?' she asked.

When I had arrived that morning, she'd told me she wasn't going to interfere or say anything because it was her husband's day to tidy.

'Very ... slowly,' I said with a wry smile. I glanced at my watch. It was already past three.

'No matter how many times I've asked him, he has never managed to tidy up his study. I'm counting on you, Miko.'

'I hope I can live up to your expectations.' Fatigue overtook me, and I sank onto the chair with a sigh. I sipped the tea, then bit into one of the ohagi. 'Delicious,' I exclaimed. The gentle sweetness of the adzuki beans permeated my body, recharging my energy. I'll have another, I thought, but when I looked at the plate, it was empty. Beside me, Hako was munching away with his lid flapping. I glared at him, and he hastily shut his lid and pretended to be an ordinary box.

My assistant is a little box who happens to love sweet adzuki beans. But who would ever believe me? I sipped my tea while dreaming of the day I'd finally get to share my secret with someone. After I'd drained my cup, I took a deep breath and rose from my chair, ready to get back to work.

'Good luck,' Mrs Midorikawa said. 'He has a lot of unfinished business.'

I bobbed my head and went back upstairs. Her words, which had seemed pregnant with meaning, were ringing in my ears. As I approached the study, I could hear the books still belting out their songs. I hurried up the last few stairs. I had a bad feeling about this.

In the middle of the towering high-rises sat Mr Midorikawa, lost in a book.

I knew it! Hako wailed. *That's why tidying books is so hazardous.*

I shut his lid sharply and said, 'Mr Midorikawa, no reading books while tidying. That's the rule.'

'Oh, sorry.' He closed the book with a sheepish look, like a child who has been caught doing something naughty. 'I hadn't seen this one for ages, so I thought I'd take a little peek.'

'You can tell which ones to keep just by touching them. Reading won't help. You need to listen to your body. I'd like you to imagine shelves lined only with books you truly love.'

'But this was given to me by a friend. It seems sort of rude to throw it away without reading it.'

'Did it spark joy when you touched it?'

He groaned as if in confusion.

'Here. Give it to me,' I said. Having lost my temper, I spoke a little shortly. I took the compilation of essays and slapped the cover with my palm.

'What are you doing?'

'Waking it up. If a book or object is in a deep sleep, it's easier to tell whether it sparks joy or not if you wake it up first. Here, why don't you try it?'

He looked dubious, but took the book and slapped it.

'What do you think? Does it spark joy?'

'No ... not at all. Even though I told my friend I wanted it.'

The book had stopped singing. It had probably got so tired it had quit trying. 'If so, then it's lost its flavour.'

'Lost its flavour?'

'The person who read it first has already absorbed all the flavour and nutrients from it.'

'You mean like bonito flakes after they've been boiled to make soup stock?'

'Yes. That happens with books, too.'

'You certainly say some interesting things. Like bonito flakes, huh?' With a sad smile, he placed the book his friend had given him on the discard pile.

For the next three hours, Mr Midorikawa worked at his own pace, sorting the books piled on the floor into those that brought joy and those that didn't. As he tidied, the shape of what he really wanted became clearer. Hidden within that sea of longing, he uncovered, one by one, what it was he really wanted to have, to do and to be. In the end, he was left with only half the volumes he'd started with, and the cacophony of voices had settled into a gentle harmony.

'Miko, what should I do next?'

'Now that you've decided which books bring you joy, you can sort them into categories and put them back on the shelves. Fiction can be organised by author, while other books can be stored together by type, such as business books, manga and magazines, as well as reference books, cookbooks, and photo and art catalogues.'

Together, we sorted the books by category and moved them from the floor to the shelves, breaking into a sweat as we went along. The bookshelves quickly filled up, until all that was left on the floor was an impressive collection of travel guides. They started with London, Paris and Spain and travelled via Egypt, Turkey, India and Beijing to Hawaii, Los Angeles and Mexico, finally ending up on the other side of the globe in Brazil. When placed together, it was like a trip around the world.

Each guidebook was humming music from its own country. Rock, chanson, flamenco, hula, salsa, samba. Music from around the world mingled in the now-tidy study, resulting in an odd ensemble. It was a lively yet slightly incongruous scene. Why, I wondered, had he kept these old guidebooks?

The Singing Study

'Not content with a correspondence education school, huh?' Hako grumbled. *'Is he planning to start a travel agency too?'*

As if he'd heard Hako, Mr Midorikawa said, 'I actually wanted to throw these away because they're quite old, but ...'

'They bring you joy, don't they?' I said, looking into his face.

'Mmm,' he nodded.

'Then that means they're important.'

'Because I have a lot of memories of my travels,' he said. 'Especially my first trip to New York.' He picked up a dog-eared guide of New York from a pile on the floor. He had a total of thirty-three guidebooks on New York alone. As we lined them up side by side on the shelf, I could hear the bustling of the city streets along with strains of jazz.

'When I was a university student, I saved up money from my part-time job delivering newspapers and went to New York.' Mr Midorikawa had a faraway look in his eyes. 'I was amazed by the skyscrapers when I first saw them. I couldn't believe there were so many. And the city looked so beautiful, wrapped in mist rising from underground. A musician was playing a saxophone on the street corner. I was so captivated, I went back many times.'

He placed the last New York guidebook on the shelf. As he did so, another book, yellowed with age, slipped out from between its pages.

'You dropped something,' I said. I picked up the slim volume and dusted it off, then handed it to Mr Midorikawa. At that moment, I thought I heard someone singing the sentimental Japanese ballads known as *enka*. These mingled with the jazz to make a peculiar chorus.

'Well, that sure brings back memories,' Mr Midorikawa murmured as he gazed at the cover.

'What is it?' I asked.

His eyes still fixed on the book, he said, 'It's one my father gave me the first time I went to New York.'

'You were going to New York and he gave you this?' I couldn't help laughing.

The cover displayed the title in elegant gilt-tooled script – *Miyamoto Musashi*. A biography of the renowned seventeenth-century samurai swordsman and philosopher.

'I know,' Mr Midorikawa said. 'Why on earth would he give me a book about Musashi? My father was a real spoilsport, never able to take a hint. Although he was a

Japanese language teacher, he was rigid, stubborn and boring. He couldn't hold his drink either, and would always sing *enka* when he was drunk. I hated those things about him and went to New York because I wanted to experience a different world. He was so upset when I told him. He insisted it was too dangerous and warned me that I would just get shot by gangs. But he finally gave in. *Miyamoto Musashi* was his parting gift.'

Mr Midorikawa gave a wry smile as he gently stroked the yellowed cover. The more he touched it, the more the memories seemed to come flooding back.

'When I think about it, he probably intended it as a kind of protective charm. If I was going to face the guns of New York gangs, then Musashi, who could wield two swords at once, was the answer. Pretty silly, really. But so like him. In the end, I got homesick after five days and started reading it on the balcony of my cheap lodgings while listening to jazz from the street below. It was so engrossing I couldn't put it down.'

'What a lovely memory,' I said. My eyes narrowed as I pictured the scene he'd described. Clearly, this slim little book was packed with memories that sparked joy.

'Every time we've moved, this book has resurfaced.

Each time I was going to throw it away, but somehow couldn't. And I would end up reading it again.'

He has a lot of unfinished business. The words of Mrs Midorikawa came back to me now. I gazed at the dog-eared book. 'Mr Midorikawa,' I said. 'Do you remember I told you that some books lose their flavour?'

'Like dried bonito flakes after making soup stock?'

'Yes, but there are also books whose flavour never changes no matter how many times you read them. In fact, the flavour only deepens.'

'Like dried squid. The more you chew it, the more you can taste it.' As he spoke, his face suddenly screwed up, as if he was desperately trying to hold back all the memories welling up inside. 'My father died of cancer last month. In the end, I never managed to thank him. I couldn't even talk to him properly. I kept avoiding him because I couldn't stand watching him grow weaker. He passed away before I got up the courage to speak with him.'

A teardrop fell on the cover, blurring the title. Hunched over, as though trying to suppress his regrets, Mr Midorikawa wept. Tears ran down his glasses and dripped onto the worn cover.

'I think I know why I asked you to come, Miko.' His

voice was trembling. 'Because I wanted to find this book again. I wanted to see my father one last time, to talk with him. But I didn't have the confidence to do that on my own. I think that's why.'

He rose slowly and wiped his eyes. 'Thank you for today.'

'It's me who should be thanking you,' I said, beaming at him. Beside me, Hako, his mouth (or rather, his lid) still smeared with adzuki bean paste, sniffed back tears.

There are times when tidying that, in the midst of all our things, we run across traces of a loved one who has gone. I believe it's because those memories want to reach us, rather than remain buried under a heap of stuff. The process of tidying opens our minds so those memories can live on in our hearts.

Mr Midorikawa placed *Miyamoto Musashi*, the last book remaining, beside the row of thirty-three New York travel guides. It should have looked awkward and out of place, but somehow it fit perfectly, as if that's where it belonged.

ROOM 3
The Bickering Kitchen

Fumi Akai (age 36) and Junpei Akai (age 38)

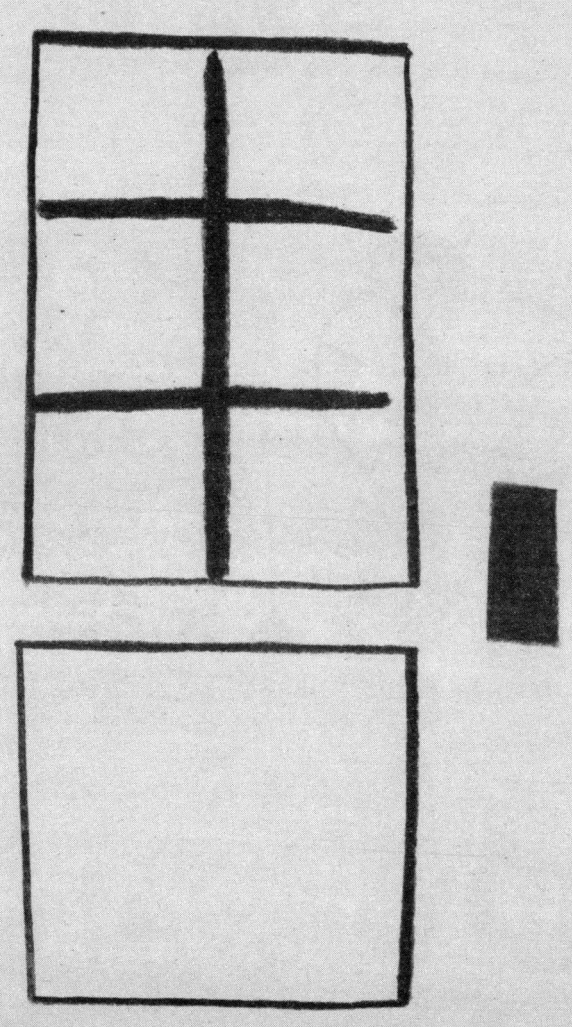

'There's no need to get so grumpy. Have a sweet. Scowling like that'll just give you frown lines.'

'Quit making me scowl then! You're the one who's making me grumpy!'

'What's the big deal, Fumi? It's just a little tidying up.'

'Just? You're so lazy you haven't even started, Junpei.' Fumi had been fuming at her husband for some time, and her face was now the colour of her red apron.

Junpei, who was still in his pyjamas and clearly had bedhead, had been taking Fumi's complaints quietly, but at this his face flushed, too. 'Who're you calling lazy? Try saying that again!'

Their silhouettes were almost identical in shape, and I couldn't help thinking they looked like stand-up comedians as they argued back and forth in Kansai dialect. Hako seemed to think so too. *Hey, Miko, when're they going to get to the punchline?* he whispered.

'Very funny,' I said. 'Although maybe you're right. It's a little easier to take if I think of it as comedy ...'

With my sassy little sidekick under one arm, I led the still quibbling couple into the red-tiled kitchen at the far end of their little house. In the crowded cupboard above the sink, the dishes were arguing just as heatedly as the couple.

You cheap old mugs! Get out of my way! shouted a wine glass surrounded by cups in the back of the cupboard.

Ha! You think you're so classy, retorted a well-used mug in the front row. *If you don't like it, you should try harder to be used more often.*

Pipe down, would you? rattled the small plates piled beside the mug. *You guys are so noisy!*

I opened a drawer. Sure enough, tins of corned beef were picking on a half-empty jar of Chinese chilli bean paste. *Disgraceful! You've only been used once and already you're out of date! How long are you planning to hang around?*

The chilli bean paste wasn't going to take these comments lying down. *You've got some nerve!* it shouted. *You'll be headed for the garbage soon without ever being tasted.*

A package of powdered Japanese soup stock, which had been eyeing this altercation disapprovingly, made

The Bickering Kitchen

a desperate appeal. *Those guys are all high-calorie. Choose me instead.*

Hako glanced around the room and laughed. *They behave like China, America and Japan at an international summit.*

'True. Everything's behaving just like this couple, fighting all the time.' My guess was that Fumi and Junpei had each filled the shelves with their own favourite things, and these had split into opposing sides. I've helped over a thousand people to tidy their homes. Every time I do, it makes me think it's not just people who inhabit a home, but also the things they own. And possessions side with their owners.

'Oh, wow. Look at all this stuff.' Fumi ran a hand through her bleached brown hair and stared at all the things jammed into the cupboards and drawers. 'We have so much. What should we do, Miko?'

'The same thing you did when tidying your clothes and books,' I said. 'Start by taking everything out. Then touch each item to see if it sparks joy. Keep those that do, and let go of those that don't. Because this is the kitchen, you're bound to find things that are past their expiry date, too. This is a good chance to discard them.'

'All right.' Fumi tied her apron tighter. 'Hey Junpei,' she said. 'Start tidying up, would you!'

'It's got nothing to do with me,' Junpei retorted, looking quite cross. He plonked himself onto the sofa in the living room beside the kitchen and switched on a comedy programme.

'Geez! What an attitude!'

Fumi looked like she was about to launch into him again, and I tugged her sleeve. 'Remember what I told you,' I urged. 'Let's start by tidying your own things.'

'But this clutter is practically a hundred per cent his fault, you know.'

'I can understand how frustrated you must feel. Many people feel that way about their family. They think, "Why am I the only one who tidies up? Why doesn't my family help?" But it's really important not to force tidying on others. We should focus on our own stuff and keep quiet. No scolding, no sarcasm, no meddling.'

'If I don't say anything, he'll never change. He hasn't even tidied up his clothes or books yet.'

'Trust me and give it a try. We can't make other people change. So there's no point in pushing them to tidy. Start with your own things. Identify which ones don't spark joy for you, and discard them.'

'Fine then. The first thing I'm getting rid of is him!' said Fumi, directing her voice towards Junpei where he sat watching TV.

Nice shot! Hako chuckled, his laughter mingling with that from the TV programme. I surveyed the cluttered kitchen and retied my neckerchief. 'Let's get to work!' I said.

Fumi and I opened the cupboards and drawers one by one and put their contents on the dining table.

Wha? 'S bright... A cup, still in its gift box and barely able to speak, squinted against the light.

Gosh, I'm so sleepy. A large plate at the very bottom of a pile yawned as if it was waking up for the first time in years.

What's this? Is it finally my turn? asked a cocktail shaker that had been waiting stoically despite rarely being used.

%&$#&%$#!! Chopsticks, forks, knives and spoons popped out one after the other uttering unintelligible words.

The dining table was soon buried under an array of dishes, and we had to start laying things out on the floor. Arguments were breaking out all over. While keeping an ear open for any problems, I began tackling the pantry. Cans of corn shouted, competing for my attention.

Hurry up and eat me!

No, me! Eat me!

Over here! Over here!

Herbs and seasonings stuffed into bags kept sneezing and coughing. Half-used bottles of oil, sauces and soy sauce, most of them no longer recognisable, groaned. *Argh. Ooh. Ugh.*

Hako held his nose, or rather his lid, as he didn't have a nose to hold. *This kitchen's so bloated, it'll be hard to slim down*, he remarked.

Fumi surveyed the volume of stuff and burst out laughing. 'Look at all this. Maybe I should open a shop!'

One reason I have my clients take everything out at once is so they can get a grasp on what they actually possess. Fumi and Junpei had bought items without consulting each other. Added up, they came to a lot.

Among the dishes and foodstuffs lined up on the floor were plastic bottle caps with little figurines on them, single-serving jam and pudding jars whose current purpose was unclear, a broken mixer and a large can of protein powder that had hardly been used. Without hesitation, Fumi began sorting these into bags for recycling and disposal.

Junpei, who had wandered unnoticed into the kitchen, rushed over and began pulling things out. 'Hey! What are you doing? Don't throw things away without asking!'

Fumi couldn't conceal her irritation. 'What's got into you all of a sudden? You don't even use them.'

'I bought this blender because you said you wanted it.'

'It was so cheap it broke right away. And I'm chucking this protein stuff because you never drink it.' She grabbed the silver can from her husband.

'Well, I'm going to start drinking it from now on. It's a waste to throw it away.'

'What's the point in building muscle when you need to lose weight first? And what about these empty jars? You're never going to use them, right? Or these bottle caps with figurines.'

'I might use them someday. And if those caps become valuable, we could sell them.'

Hako frowned as he watched them argue. *Here they go again. The husband-and-wife stand-up routine. Can't you stop them, Miko?*

'Excuse me,' I said, stepping between them. 'Fumi, please leave Junpei's things for him to sort himself.' I turned to Junpei. 'Perhaps you could consider parting with things that don't bring you joy. Isn't it more of a waste to spend your time wondering what to do with all these things or feeling like they're in the way?'

'I'll never agree to get rid of something that can still be used. We'll just end up buying the same thing again anyway.'

I sighed. I guess I tried that angle too soon, I thought. Junpei had been like this ever since I'd arrived. The enormous sock collection in the wardrobe, the broken radio hidden among the books, never-used guest futon

The Bickering Kitchen

shoved in a closet, a foam massage roller, yoga mat and dumbbells bought during a health craze and quickly abandoned in the entranceway, a stock of towels piled beside the bathroom sink.

Every time Fumi tried to discard something, Junpei would appear and stop her, saying, 'We might be able to use it.' For him, whether something sparked joy or not appeared to be irrelevant. He wanted to keep everything. To be interrupted yet again when she was trying to tidy the kitchen was more than Fumi could take.

'Why don't you just shut up and watch TV? If you've got enough time to butt in, go throw away the CDs and DVDs in that bookcase you never tidied. You don't need them. You can listen to music and watch movies online.'

'It costs money to do anything online. And what about you? You've got all that make-up stuff even

though it doesn't make a bit of difference, no matter how much you use.'

'If you aren't going to tidy, just leave me alone! You're the first thing I'm going to chuck!' Having lost her last shred of patience, Fumi began throwing all the expired foodstuffs into the garbage bag. Taken aback by her ferocious scowl, Junpei returned glumly to the sofa.

'Why does he feel so strongly about these things?' I asked Fumi before I could stop myself.

'He didn't used to be like this,' she murmured, glancing to where he sat hunched over, watching TV. 'He began hoarding things after the disaster.'

'Disaster?'

'The 2011 earthquake and tsunami in Tohoku. He'd been posted there and was living on his own. The disaster itself was terrifying enough, but then afterwards, it was a struggle to get enough food and essentials because the shops were empty. Ever since, he keeps stocking up on things and hoarding.'

Many people who've experienced emergency situations such as earthquakes, fires and pandemics start hoarding. It's natural to want to prepare for future disasters. But overstocking and hoarding can make daily life much harder. In my tidying work, I've come across some astonishing stockpiles – dozens of boxes of plastic wrap, hundreds of toilet-paper rolls, thousands of masks. At such times, I recommend counting each item, then calculating how long it will take to use up what's there. This makes it clear that we could never consume it all even in ten or twenty years.

'When you're stocking up on something,' I told Fumi, 'it's helpful to make a mental note of how many of that item is equivalent to a week's, or a month's supply. Based on that, you can decide the maximum number to keep on hand and set a clear limit on the amount of storage space allotted to it. When we're surrounded with things we can't use up, life feels cramped.'

I grabbed a large handful of chopsticks from the pile in which there must have been over thirty pairs. 'You have two children, so you're a family of four, right? How many guests come for dinner at one time? If you count them, you'll know how many pairs are enough. Counting helps us to avoid buying more than we need.'

'You're right,' said Fumi, as she chose ten pairs of chopsticks from the pile.

Next, she pulled open the kitchen's last bastion:

The Bickering Kitchen

the freezer compartment of the fridge. A snow-white world emerged with a scraping sound. I took out a frost-rimmed Tupperware filled with 'something'.

I-I'm c-cold. Whatever was inside that container was shivering.

'What's ... this?' I asked.

'Hmm. I wonder.' Fumi scraped off the frost. 'Looks like ... curry,' she said with an embarrassed laugh.

'From when?'

'Maybe three years ago. The kids liked sweet curry when they were younger, and I used to make extra and freeze it.'

'It's hard to throw away something you worked hard to make, isn't it?'

'But it's three years old. No one can eat it now.' She threw it away and continued her exploration of the freezer compartment. One by one, dormant items appeared. A pile of freezer packs, containers of frozen rice, pure white pie sheets. All of them complained that they were 'freezing'.

It's like exploring the Antarctic, Hako grumbled, his breath puffing out white clouds.

As if she had heard what Hako said, Fumi muttered, 'I suppose I can't really judge my husband, can I?'

Whispering Rooms

While Fumi was dealing with the things in the freezer, I began working on the vegetable drawer. I pulled out an enamel container that had been stored deep inside. 'What's this, Fumi?' I asked.

'Oh, that's miso. I haven't seen that in quite a while.'

'Miso! How old is it?' I stared at the container which looked as if it could hold about three kilos.

'Hmm. About four years, maybe?' She laughed and opened the lid. The jar was packed full of miso which had now turned a very dark brown. 'When my mother-in-law passed away, I brought this back as a keepsake. She was a good cook, and her miso soup with tofu, made with her own homemade miso, was the best. I learned how to cook a lot of things from her.'

'What a lovely keepsake. But I guess you can't eat it anymore.'

'Actually, I'm thinking maybe we can. After all, miso is used as a preservative, too.'

'If it sparks joy, then keep it.'

There are times in tidying up when old things are not enemies but allies. What counts is whether you can find the ones that spark joy. I put the enamel container to one side and looked around the kitchen. 'You've done a great job, Fumi. The kitchen is pretty much full of things you love, don't you think?'

'That's thanks to you, Miko. Although I haven't even touched my husband's stuff.' Her gaze shifted to the pile of things still on the floor.

'That's okay. Give him time.'

All we could do was wait. But I was certain it would work out. To direct her thoughts to a more constructive topic, I said firmly, 'Time to start storing!'

'So how should I go about it?' Fumi asked. 'If I'm not careful, I'll just end up right back where I started.'

'With this type of kitchen, I recommend storing pots and pans under the sink and seasonings and foodstuffs under the range. Any dishes that are in boxes should be taken out and placed on the shelves above the counter.' I pointed to each spot as I explained. 'You can store things to create a rainbow in your kitchen.'

'A – rainbow?'

Oh boy, here we go. Miko's rainbow, said Hako, rolling his eyes. *How many times do I have to tell you? No one's going to understand if you don't explain.*

Glancing at the preachy little box out of the corner of my eye, I went on. 'Store similar things side by side. For example, storage items like Tupperware containers go with jars, and chopstick holders go with chopsticks. Store them to create harmony among the diverse array of items and arrange them like you would a gradation of colour, as if you were painting a rainbow.'

Fumi began putting the pots and pans under the sink. By the time she'd finished putting everything away, all the items she'd chosen to keep looked somehow pleased and proud.

But when we launched into storing the foodstuffs, we immediately ran into a wicker basket stuffed to the brim with teabags. There were English teabags chatting in a sophisticated tone, oolong teabags speaking rapid-fire Chinese, green teabags murmuring confidentially, and beneath them, husky-voiced *genmaicha* teabags gossiping idly.

'What should I do with these, Miko?'

I motioned to Hako with my eyes. He opened his lid reluctantly, and I reached in and removed several smaller boxes. 'Just like with clothes and books, store everything upright,' I said. 'That's the one thing I'm very particular about in my approach to storage. Clothes that have been folded should be stored upright in the chest of drawers or clothes cases. Pens, pencils and other stationery tools should also be placed vertically in the drawer. Most storage problems can be solved simply by storing things upright.'

As I spoke, I placed all the teabags upright in the little boxes. Fumi watched me restore order to the messy mound as if I was performing a magic show. I noticed that Junpei was also watching me from his vantage point on the sofa. Almost there, I whispered to myself.

'I also recommend removing any prices or labels. That includes discount labels or *Buy one, get one free!* stickers. Too much written information in the kitchen is disturbing. By eliminating unnecessary information, you can create a more serene atmosphere. And not just in the kitchen but in the whole house.'

Fumi began ripping off labels and soon, the noisy kitchen had quieted down. 'You were right,' she said. 'Those labels made the kitchen too busy.' She looked pleased as her eyes took in the tidy kitchen.

'You can do the same thing with many other things, too, like dehumidifiers, deodorisers and detergents,' I said. 'Try it out.'

'All right. I guess all that's left is the stove and sink area, right? I'm not sure how to tackle it though.'

'A lot of people feel that way. Often there are pots and pans left on the burners, and bottles of seasonings sticky with grease. Dishes that have been washed are often still in the dish rack and the bottom of the dish detergent bottle may be slimy with mould.'

'Sounds like my kitchen. So what should I do?'

'I recommend rethinking the whole premise of kitchen storage. Instead of focusing on storage methods, focus

The Bickering Kitchen

on ease of cleaning. In the end, this means not leaving anything out on the counter near the sink or stovetop. Keep everything you need stored out of sight and bring things out only when you need them. It's quite addicting because it feels so wonderful to be able to clean your kitchen quickly and easily.'

The only things remaining on the table were the dishes, and these no longer argued because Fumi had kept just the ones that sparked joy. Instead, they waited quietly to be stored.

'They're all awake now, aren't they?'

'What d'you mean?' Fumi asked.

'Dishes removed from the shelves suddenly become visible, as if they're emerging from hibernation.'

'That's true. I didn't even realise I had a lot of these.' She picked up a large Scandinavian platter that had been kept in a wooden box, then examined a pair of rice bowls fired in a kiln in Kyushu and lacquered bowls from the Hokuriku region in Northwest Japan famed for its lacquerware. 'These are all exquisite, but I'd forgotten they were even there. I set them aside for special occasions because it seemed a waste to use them just for us.'

People often keep their best dishes on the shelf and choose giveaways or cheap dishes from dollar shops for daily use. But dishes that are only taken out occasionally for guests gradually lose their inherent lustre.

'You should use your good dishes as much as possible. Restaurants in Kyoto routinely serve food on expensive dishes. If you want a lifestyle that sparks joy, use beautiful things every day.'

'I guess you're right,' Fumi whispered, as she stroked one of the rice bowls.

'Why not start now?' I suggested.

'Huh?'

'It's almost lunchtime.'

'So it is. I'll put the rice on.' Fumi's glance fell on the enamel container I'd put in a corner of the room. 'Maybe I'll try using that four-year-old miso too.'

We stood side by side in the tidy kitchen preparing lunch. We washed the rice and cooked it in an earthenware pot. While waiting for it to cook, we made soup stock from dried kelp, cut up some tofu and opened the lid of the enamel container in which Fumi's mother-in-law had kept her homemade miso. The smell of fermented soybeans filled the kitchen. The aroma was so soothing I was sure that Fumi's mother-in-law had been a very kind person. Fumi took a spoon and scooped up a little, licking it timidly with her tongue. Hako cracked his lid open to keep an eye on her.

Yikes! he said anxiously. *Is she going to be okay? What if she gets food poisoning?*

'How is it?'

Fumi smiled. 'Mm. Still tastes good.'

Drawn by the familiar scent, Junpei rose slowly from the sofa. He wandered into the kitchen, patting ineffectually at his cowlick as though embarrassed by his bedhead, and stopped in front of his pile of things on the floor. He crouched down and began sorting through them.

Fumi, who was stirring miso into the pot of steaming soup, flicked her eyes at me, as if to say, 'Look at that!' I smiled back at her from the sink where I was washing the cutting board. Just as I thought: my strategy had succeeded.

The desire to tidy up usually doesn't occur in two people at the same time. Many people feel disgruntled when they begin, wondering why their family won't help make their home a tidier place.

Houses remind me of a seesaw. Built level to the ground, a house, as well as the people who live in it, will always seek the point of equilibrium. When one spouse reduces the volume of their possessions, it's as if the house has tilted, and this causes the other spouse to begin tidying up without being asked. The rest of the family start taking an interest, too. I frequently witness how tidying sets off a chain reaction. This is why I advise my clients not to nag or get sarcastic with other family members, but instead to quietly get on with their own tidying. I call this the 'sun strategy' after Aesop's fable about the north wind and the sun. If we start taking action instead of letting ourselves be irritated by someone else's behaviour, the other person will begin to change. It will also help us see their strengths and weaknesses and how we can relate to them better. Maybe this applies not just to tidying, but to life as well.

Junpei finished sorting through his things in no time. Almost everything ended up in the rubbish, but his expression was sunny. Just as he finished cleaning the floor, bowls filled with freshly cooked rice were placed on the table. Beside each was a bowl of miso soup with tofu flavoured with four-year-old miso.

'Looks delicious.' Junpei smiled as if lost in memories.

'Why don't you eat with us?' Fumi said. 'This pair of rice bowls and the miso in the soup are from your mother.'

Still in his PJs, Junpei ducked his head apologetically. 'Fumi, I'm sorry. I'll tidy up properly from now on.'

'No worries, Junpei. Let's eat. Can't do much on an empty stomach, can we?'

We sat at the table, placed our palms together and said *'Itadakimasu!'* In addition to the rice and miso soup, our lunch featured rice bran pickles and pickled plums, both of which had been found in the fridge. We each cracked an egg into our bowls of hot rice and mixed it together with soy sauce until the rice was smooth and fluffy.

The four-year-old miso gave the soup a rich and subtle flavour that seeped into my body. The red-tiled kitchen was clear of clutter, and the clamour of competing voices was gone. Instead, all the things in the kitchen were chatting amicably as if they were in some delightful restaurant.

At the dining table beside the kitchen, Fumi and Junpei, who'd been arguing constantly, were now quietly and companionably eating soup and rice from

matching bowls. Catching sight of the smile on my face as I watched them, Fumi leaned over and whispered in my ear, 'The miso turned out to be pretty good, so I've decided to hang on to Junpei a little longer and see if the flavour deepens with age.'

ROOM 4
The Silent Childhood Bedroom

Saori Shimon (age 21)

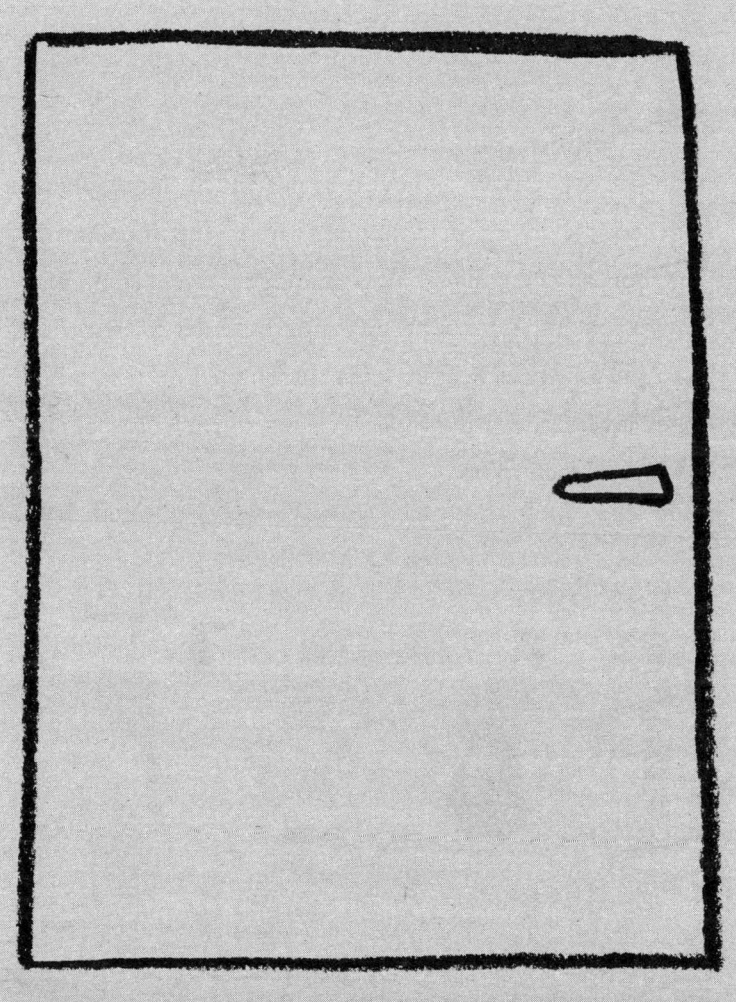

Rooms are chatty. They tell me much more about the people living in a home than if the inhabitants introduced themselves. They get angry, weep, laugh and yawn. I help people set their homes in order so that they can pursue their ideal lifestyle surrounded only by what they love. As we tidy, I like to listen to the voices of the things in each room.

The Silent Childhood Bedroom

But Saori Shimon's room was silent.

'To be honest, I don't know what to take with me,' she mumbled, ducking her head apologetically.

She hasn't stopped apologising since we got here, Miko, Hako said, peering at her through his lid.

Sorry it's such a mess. Sorry I'm so inefficient. Sorry I can't make up my mind.

Her ponytail swayed with each apologetic bob of her head. Although with her childlike face she looked to be only in her mid-teens, she'd recently graduated from university and was about to start working. She was moving out of her childhood home to a place near her company, and her new life would begin tomorrow.

'There's no need to apologise, Saori,' I said, trying to encourage her. 'Take your time. Touch each item and choose the ones that spark joy.'

At that moment, her mother, Yukiko, opened the door. 'How's it going?' she asked. She wore a long black dress identical to the one Saori had on. Yukiko's eyes fell on the piles of clothing on the floor. Tucking her neatly cropped shoulder-length hair behind her ears, she exclaimed, 'Saori, you've hardly made any progress at all! You better try harder than that.'

It was Yukiko, not Saori, who had asked me to come. The very first thing Yukiko had told me when I arrived at the apartment that morning was: 'Saori's starting work tomorrow, but she can't do anything without my help. She can't even tidy up her own room.'

'Maybe I should give you a hand after all,' Yukiko said.

'No, we're fine!' I said quickly, intercepting her as she moved eagerly into the room. 'It may take a little while, but I can assure you that Saori will be able to tidy up on her own.'

There's no point in tidying unless you do it yourself. Because the purpose is to discover what sparks joy for you.

Geez! Talk about overprotective, Hako whispered with a frown.

At her mother's appearance, Saori had clammed up completely. I tried to encourage her. 'Saori, think of tidying as a festival and enjoy it! After all, moving is the perfect chance to tidy up.'

'A festival?' Saori raised her head for the first time.

'That's right. The best way to approach tidying is to have fun, just like you would at a festival! You have to

The Silent Childhood Bedroom

take everything out to move anyway, so it's easy to look at each thing you own and decide what you want to take with you.'

Saori smiled, as if she'd seen a ray of hope. 'Maybe you're right,' she said.

'My tidying method is like a mini-move. Moving is a chance to create a new lifestyle. An opportunity to graduate from who you are now and choose the kind of energy and components you want in your life. It's the best time to let go of things that don't bring you joy, like accessories you never wear, presents you've left in a drawer, or letters from an old boyfriend, and begin a new life.'

I smiled at Saori, and she smiled back. 'Unfortunately, I don't have any letters from an old boyfriend,' she said, 'but I'll give it a try.'

Encouraged, she reached out and picked up a black pleated skirt. I pricked up my ears, but the skirt said nothing. The rest of her clothes also remained silent, as if resigned to not being chosen. 'How does it feel? Does it spark joy?'

'Um, well, it's still new, but somehow it feels a bit stiff.'

'If it doesn't give you a thrill, then let it go,' I urged her. She folded it lightly and put it on the pile of clothes she was discarding.

'Hold on, Saori!' said Yukiko, who was watching from the sidelines. She picked up the skirt and spread it out. 'This is one I picked for you, isn't it? It's still in perfectly good condition. It would be a shame to get rid of it.'

'Mm ... I guess you're right. It's easy to match with other things so I suppose I might wear it sometimes.' Just like that, Saori changed her mind.

Yukiko placed the skirt against Saori's waist. 'See! It suits you really well.' She put it on the pile of things Saori had decided to keep.

Like a comedy duo in perfect sync, Hako and I almost fell over in exasperation. *Oh-oh. I don't like the looks of this*, Hako muttered, popping his lid open a crack. For once, we were in perfect agreement. I knew from experience that this was heading in a bad direction.

'Oh! Are you throwing this out too?' Yukiko took a white shirt dress off the discard pile.

'Oh, sorry, Mum,' Saori said contritely.

'How could you? This is one of my favourites that I used to wear.' Once again, Yukiko placed the garment

The Silent Childhood Bedroom

against Saori and examined how it looked. 'It's so elegant. It's perfect for you.'

'Yes, Mum. I must have put it on that pile by mistake.'

'Excuse me,' I said. Now that I'd seen how easily Saori was swayed by her mother's words, it was time to intervene. 'I'm so sorry, Mrs Shimon, but would you mind stepping out of the room for a little while?'

'Oh dear, am I in the way?'

Finally got the hint, did you? Darn right you're in the way! Hako growled from his position under my arm.

I pressed his lid shut and bowed to Saori's mother. 'If Saori is to start a new life, she needs to choose on her own,' I said. 'It would help if you could give us a little more time to work on this together.'

'Oh, yes, of course. That's why I hired you after all. Sorry to interrupt. Please help Saori make up her mind.' She tucked her straight black hair behind her ears again and left the room rather reluctantly. The way she looked at her daughter was reminiscent of a mother worrying about a small child, and I guessed she'd looked at Saori that way ever since she was born.

We should never let our family see what we discard. It's particularly stressful for parents to watch. Throwing

away plushies and clothes our parents gave us is a sign of maturation, a step towards independence. While this new-found independence brings our parents joy, it can also make them sad. That's why many parents make their children feel guilty, pressing them to keep unnecessary items by telling them it's a waste to throw those things away.

'Now how do you feel about that white shirt dress? Does it bring you joy?'

'I wonder,' Saori answered uncertainly. 'You know what Mum said.' Yukiko's intervention seemed to have robbed Saori of her ability to decide. She'd probably always believed that her mother's opinion was right.

The Silent Childhood Bedroom

The room was silent as usual. Clothes, books, furniture. All of the things in her room waited quietly, watching Saori with the same questioning gaze Saori always fixed on her mother. I guessed this was because it was her mother who had picked them all. They'd been chosen from motherly longings. Things like 'This will look good on her' and 'I hope she'll become this kind of person.' The reason Saori couldn't decide was because she'd never chosen anything based on what she herself loved.

Now Saori was as silent as her room. 'From my own experience,' I told her, 'daughters rarely keep wearing clothes chosen for them by their mothers. But for that very reason, they usually can't throw those clothes away either.'

It's hard for children to know what brings them joy if their parents choose everything for them before they've developed their own joy criteria. This is probably true not just for choosing things, but also for making other decisions in our lives.

In the past, I used to 'give' my clothes to my younger sister. I thought I was being kind, but when I became a tidying consultant, I realised I was fooling myself. Far from being kind, I was forcing my sister to bear the guilt of having to discard my things.

Saori spread out the shirt dress her mother had passed on to her. 'It seems a shame to throw this away,' she said, as if defending her mother. 'Perhaps I could use it for loungewear?'

'I'm afraid that's not a good solution either, Saori. Nine out of ten outfits demoted to loungewear are never worn. Most clients I've met already have so much demoted loungewear they don't know what to do with it. I can tell quite easily what sorts of things they wear at home because loungewear influences the way people look when they go out. If you wear demoted garments that don't spark joy inside, it will show in your behaviour and your lifestyle. You should wear clothes

The Silent Childhood Bedroom

that spark joy even when you're at home. It raises your self-esteem, too.'

'I envy you.'

'Me?'

'You know exactly what you like and your job is something you love doing.'

'I wasn't like this from the start, you know. It took me quite some time to realise what I really wanted to do.' As I said this, I recalled Yukiko's anxious words when she'd asked me to help Saori get ready to move. *She won't be able to live on her own. I've told her that so many times.*

But maybe Saori wanted to use her first job as an opportunity to start changing. If so, I wanted to help her. I pulled myself together and said, 'Let's get back to tidying!'

'I'm not sure what to do next.' Saori looked around the white room. Although larger than average, the room's layout was typical of many children's rooms, with a bed against the far wall, a closet to the left and a desk and bookcase on the right. But it didn't feel at all like a child's room because everything in it, including the walls and the furniture, were gradations of white, black and grey.

'We'll tidy by category,' I said. 'Once we finish your clothes, we'll move on to books and papers and then miscellaneous items. We'd better get as much done as possible before your mother comes back.'

'Right!'

We both laughed as we got back to work, dividing up the jobs. While Saori sorted through the rest of her clothes, I took all the books off the shelves. Even when I held them, I couldn't hear the usual singsong voices I associate with books. I guessed that Saori's mother had chosen these, too. Soon they were all on the floor.

Earlier I'd noticed a yellow toy box in the closet, so I pulled it out and opened the lid. In the silent room, the plink-plink of a toy piano sounded. A toy monkey clashed its symbols together and the delicate strains of 'Over the Rainbow' rose from a music box.

'My mother often bought me toys when I was little,' said Saori as she came up beside me and peered into the box. The sounds seemed to have switched on her memories.

'They're all wonderful,' I said. I couldn't help thinking that the yellow toy box looked very out of place in this room.

Mummy, let's sing together, the toy piano said in a childlike voice.

Listen, Mummy! said the monkey, laughing with delight. *Clash-clash.*

Mummy! Mummy! Play it again, demanded the music box.

'My father worked for a trading company and often went overseas on business trips. My mother used to buy me whatever toys I wanted so that I wouldn't feel lonely. She was a stay-at-home mum, and I was their only child. She and I used to play with these toys together all the time.'

'Your mother's very kind, isn't she?'

'Yes. Too kind, really.' Saori picked up the well-used

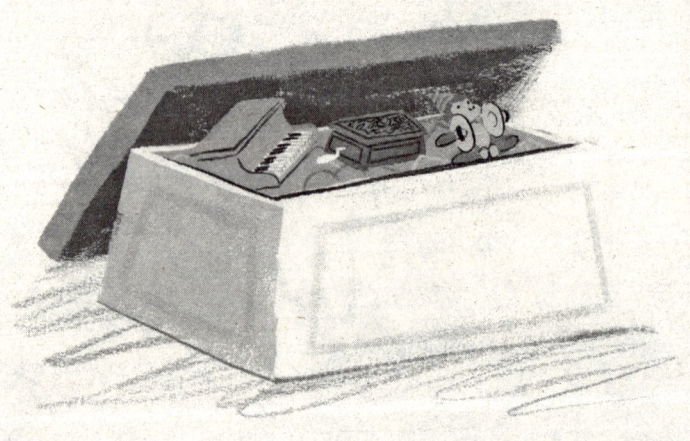

The Silent Childhood Bedroom

music box. 'She's overprotective, isn't she? I know that. Ever since I entered elementary school, I've always done whatever she said. Her words meant everything to me, whether it was about the clothes I wore, the books I read, the lessons I took or the friends I played with. I never went through a rebellious stage. I thought all I wanted was to make her happy.' She looked at the monotone clothes lying on the floor and the plain writing tools on the desk. 'When I chose books or clothes, I was always thinking, if I want this, she'll be happy. If I wear that, she won't like it.'

'Why were you so accommodating?'

'I don't know. It was like I was under some kind of spell.'

'Spell?' Surprised at her choice of words, I paused to look at her in mid-reach for a toy.

'On my seventh birthday, I begged my grandfather to buy me a dress. It was the first one I'd ever really wanted. With pink frills. What do you think my mother said when she saw it?'

'It would have made her very happy, so I guess she would have said you looked cute in it.'

Saori shook her head. 'No. She told me I'm so plain

I'd better wear clothes that look more elegant. Without realising it, I began choosing things I was sure she wouldn't object to. And always black and white, whether clothes, shoes or anything else. Although I would have loved to get pink or light blue scissors or pens, when I saw her expression, I chose black or white. I gradually convinced myself that this was what I actually liked.'

As I listened to her words, my heart constricted. Perhaps because we were close in age, I could understand her feelings to a painful degree. Like her, I'd once worn clothes that resembled a school uniform because I knew it would make my mother happy. I'd also taken private lessons and gone to the schools my mother recommended. When I started working for a publishing company, she joked about women not having to work so hard, maybe because she'd stayed home to raise me instead of working. 'Don't get a busy job,' she advised me. 'Or one that requires responsibility. You'll never get married if you do.'

For me, this wasn't funny. But in retrospect I realise that no one likes to have the path they've chosen in life criticised, and perhaps she felt that I, by working so hard, was judging her.

'We need to choose our own path in life!' I declared.

Saori cast me a puzzled expression.

There you go again, Miko, Hako said anxiously. *Don't confuse people by blurting out a thought you've been expanding inside your head!*

Although I realised I'd probably blown it again, I didn't let that stop me. 'I can understand how your mother feels when she says it's a waste,' I said. 'But I think it's even more important to know what we don't need than what we want. To know that we can live without something, rather than hanging on to it for fear we might need it someday.'

Saori nodded, then rose and began throwing clothes into a bag. To my surprise, when she was done, she had kept less than half.

'I'm going to do this,' she announced. 'I'm going to tidy up so that I can start my new life.' Her face was radiant.

When helping people tidy up, I often get to see moments like these. Bearing witness to a person's first step into their new life is one of the thrills of my job.

It was time to begin packing. I rolled up my sleeves and tightened my red neckerchief. 'Next, let's fold the clothes you've chosen to keep and pack them in cardboard boxes. Folding is an opportunity to express your love and appreciation for the clothes that support you in your life. So, when you fold them, do it with gratitude for their unfailing protection. If you do, you'll start noticing little details, like places that are threadbare or outfits that have reached the end of their life.'

'It sounds a bit like taking care of children.' Saori smiled and began carefully folding. The clothes, which up until now had been silent, began to breathe and whisper. They were trying to become hers.

'When parents express their love physically by hugging their children or patting them on the head, it's calming and reassuring. The energy that flows from the palm of our hand can help heal both mind and body. Clothes that have been properly folded will stay fresh and vibrant.'

'If that's the case, I must be pretty withered,' Saori said a little wistfully.

'What makes you say that?'

'My mum hasn't hugged me since junior high.'

The Silent Childhood Bedroom

'Mine neither, Saori. I'm guessing it was because she wanted to treat me as an adult rather than because of any ill feeling.'

Saori fell silent again. Regretting my remarks, I said brightly, 'There's a trick for packing boxes when you move.'

It took Saori a moment to respond. 'Oh, please tell me.'

'Pack your things by category. Then take them out as soon as you arrive and get rid of the cardboard boxes. Never leave your things in the box. If you do, they may still be there the next time you move.'

'Um, actually, now that you mention it, I do have a box from when we moved in here.' Saori pulled it out from deep inside the closet.

'Turn it upside down and dump everything on the floor. That will wake all the objects up, and they'll come tumbling out in surprise,' I said with a laugh.

She flipped the box over. Photos from her childhood and miscellaneous sentimental items dropped to the floor. 'You're right! It sounds like they're saying "Whoa!"'

'The point of a tidying festival is to give your life a good shake-up instead of putting life off to some unknown future date. Even the most precious things will end up in the rubbish if they're left too long in a box. You should move only after consciously selecting what you really want to take with you.'

The doorbell rang just as the rays of the late afternoon sun shone into the room. A couple of moving men in blue overalls entered. With muscled arms, they picked up the boxes and carried them away one after another. As the mountain of boxes dwindled, there appeared a red box that stood out from the rest.

'Is this yours, Saori?' I asked.

She looked a little embarrassed as she picked it up. 'Yes. It's probably the most expensive thing I've ever bought in my life.'

Really? What, what? Give us a look, will you! I struggled to keep Hako's lid on as he pushed against it, eager to take a peek. Being a box himself made him very curious to see inside.

'Don't laugh,' Saori said as she gently opened the lid.

Inside lay a pair of red high heels. 'I'm going to be working for a small movie company. The day they notified me that my application was accepted, I splurged and bought these. Don't they remind you of the ones Dorothy wore in *The Wizard of Oz*? My mother and I watched that movie over and over when I was a kid. I loved it so much I got the book and read it repeatedly. My mother has probably forgotten all about it by now, but I've always wanted a pair of ruby slippers like Dorothy's. Magic shoes that will take you anywhere when you click your heels.'

'How pretty!' I stood staring at the shoes, enchanted. She put them in my hands where they gleamed ruby red. Hako's cheeks were flushed as he gazed at them.

'I was actually offered an office job in a trading company as well. My mother recommended taking it because I'd be more likely to meet someone I could marry and have a stable income, too. But for the first time in my life, I rebelled.'

'You hit your rebellious phase a little late.'

'Yes. And I expect my mother's right. Such pretty shoes as these probably don't suit me. But ... I thought I'd wear them anyway, when I need courage.'

Let's go then, the shoes said. *We can go anywhere.* I guessed that ever since she'd bought them, Saori had been telling herself the same thing.

I pictured her choosing these shoes from those displayed in the store. I could feel how her heart sang, her breath 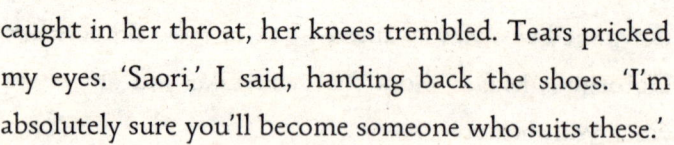 caught in her throat, her knees trembled. Tears pricked my eyes. 'Saori,' I said, handing back the shoes. 'I'm absolutely sure you'll become someone who suits these.'

'Thank you, Miko.' She hugged them to her chest and beamed at me.

The moving men returned and asked her to check what they'd packed in the truck. With my eyes, I gestured for her to go ahead, and she left the room. As soon as she'd gone, her mother came in with the vacuum cleaner.

'My goodness! It's all tidied up.' With a sad little sigh, she began vacuuming the room. From the practised way she moved, it was clear that she'd vacuumed her daughter's room like this every day. Her eyes fell on the rubbish bags outside the door. 'Look at how much she's throwing away.'

'She touched each one and kept only those that sparked joy.'

The Silent Childhood Bedroom

'I did that once, too.'

'Really?'

'Yes. About ten years ago I think. I wanted to give Saori's clothes to my niece, so I sorted through them. I took each one in my hands. It was hard to believe Saori had once worn such small things. I felt somehow forlorn and hugged them tight.'

'And did they spark joy?'

'No. The feeling I was expecting was no longer there. Her little outfits were so cute I thought I'd never want to part with them, but I realised it wasn't the clothes but Saori that I really loved. It was her I wanted to hug. Yet in the end, I kept nagging and lecturing her. I wish I'd hugged her more.'

Yukiko ran her hand over the door jamb, stroking the lines marked on it. They indicated Saori's height as she had grown.

'I think Saori knows how much you love her,' I said, looking at the lines.

'I hope so,' Yukiko murmured with a smile. 'You certainly found yourself an interesting job, Miko.'

'You mean tidying?'

'Yes. It's what I've been doing all along. If I'd been

born in a different era, I might have been able to make it my job too.'

I nodded. 'That's true.' I remembered the first day I started this job. A series of strange coincidences had led me to it.

Saori's voice pulled me from my reverie. She'd come back without me realising it. 'Well, I'm off!' she said. She bobbed her head, setting her ponytail swaying.

'Good luck, Saori,' I said, and gave her slender body a hug.

And don't apologise for things that don't matter, said Hako with a chuckle.

'Mum,' Saori said as she turned to her mother. Her eyes were no longer trying to guess what her mother wanted but instead were full of confidence. 'I'm leaving now.'

'Off you go then.'

'Could you take care of this for me?' Saori handed her the old music box we'd found. It began playing 'Over the Rainbow'.

'That's from *The Wizard of Oz*, isn't it?' said Yukiko.

Saori looked surprised. 'You remember?'

'Of course! We always watched it together, right? You loved Dorothy's ruby slippers.'

The Silent Childhood Bedroom

'Mum...' A tear ran down Saori's cheek. 'Thank you so much for everything.' She bowed low as if to hide her tears, then turned on her heel and headed for the front door.

Yukiko followed after her, gazing at her with affection. The strains of 'Over the Rainbow' rose from her hands, as if expressing grief at their parting and blessing Saori's new journey at the same time.

Saori brushed away her tears and slipped her feet into her ruby-coloured shoes. 'Bye, Mum! See you!' She clicked her heels, just like Dorothy, as if to say, 'With these shoes, I can go anywhere.'

ROOM 5
The Chatty Little Box

Miko Toboku (age 26)

How did I get started in the eccentric profession of helping people tidy up? When did I begin to hear things talk? Why do I take a chatty little box with me wherever I go?

As I said, I was led to this work by a series of strange coincidences. That makes it a long story, but I'd like to share it with you.

Even as a child, I sometimes heard things speak. The first time was when I was in elementary school. My father bought me a yellow bike for my seventh birthday. I was thrilled and rode it every day and everywhere. Three years passed, during which time I grew twenty centimetres. My yellow bike, which had once seemed so big, was now too small.

'Looks like it's time to buy you a new one,' my father said. We got on our bikes and rode off to a shop on the

The Chatty Little Box

main street. As soon as I entered, I fell in love with a sky-blue bike.

'I want that one,' I said. 'The sky-blue one.'

'It's a bit big, but it looks good to me too,' my father said. He smiled and bought it for me.

When I straddled the seat, the tyres, handles and frame seemed huge and shiny.

'Would you like us to take your old bicycle for you?' asked the shop owner.

My father looked at me and said, 'Is that okay with you?' I nodded silently.

I rode my new bike home. For some reason, I felt sad, even though I should have been ecstatic. After dinner,

I couldn't bear it anymore. I went back to the bicycle shop on my own. There was my old yellow bike in a corner of the store with a bunch of other bicycles waiting to be discarded. My old friend, which I had ridden every day, looked dull and small, as if it had died. It broke my heart to see it like that, and I ran my hand over its worn-out saddle. At that moment, I thought I heard someone sobbing. It sounded like a little girl, but it came from my old bike.

Tears welled in my eyes. 'I'm sorry,' I said over and over, stroking the saddle until the bike finally stopped crying.

Another time I remember hearing an object's voice was when I started senior high school. My mother bought me my first leather wallet – brown with white stitching on the edges. 'You're grown up now,' she said. 'You should have a proper wallet.'

I removed the bills and coins from my old vinyl wallet, as well as my train pass and bank card, and put them in the new one. As I did so, I heard a deep sigh. Surprised, I peered at my old wallet. It looked withered and deflated, as if its soul had been sucked out.

'Thank you for everything,' I whispered. I wrapped

The Chatty Little Box

it in one of my favourite hankies and put it in a drawer. From inside the hankie, I thought I heard another sigh, followed by the sound of snoring.

When I got my first job right after graduating from university, I bought a smartphone to replace my first mobile phone, which I'd got when I entered senior high. After transferring all my data, including my list of contacts, memos and photos, into the new phone, I sent a text from it to my old phone.

I typed in 'Thank you for all your hard work' and pressed 'Send.'

The old phone vibrated as the text came through. At that moment, I heard a voice whisper, *You're welcome*, and the old phone's screen went blank. No matter how many times I tried to recharge and start it, it never revived.

As I got into the habit of greeting the new and bidding farewell to the old – when replacing a worn-out handbag, switching to a new datebook or buying new socks, for instance – I was increasingly able to hear things speak to me. Perhaps as we interact with our things, the memories we share with them become like their soul or spirit, and it's this spirit that I hear speaking.

I don't think this ability is all that special. Since

ancient times Japanese people have believed myriad spirits and deities inhabit natural phenomena like trees and rocks, mountains and rivers. I'm sure the voices of these things are all around us. The only difference is whether or not a person notices.

I suppose I must sound like I live in some weird fantasy world. Hako is always telling me that. As a talking box, he's got a lot of nerve to say so.

To set your mind at rest, just let me say that I'm a very practical person and have been since childhood. I don't believe in space aliens, ghosts or fortune-telling. I love doing housework, including cooking, cleaning and laundry. Of all of these, however, my favourite has always been tidying.

I started off tidying up my own room, then reorganised my parents' and my siblings' rooms (without their permission), and went on to the kitchen, living room, laundry room and any other space I could find. Not content with tidying the house, I tackled every area in my school that I was allowed to touch. During recess, while my friends were outside playing dodgeball, I was reorganising the lockers in the classroom or returning books to their shelves in the school library. After school,

The Chatty Little Box

when everyone headed for home, I tidied up the gym equipment, the music room or the art room.

Around the time I entered senior high, however, tidying began to weigh on me. No matter how much I tidied, the reordered spaces were soon cluttered again, and I felt like I was getting nowhere. I read my mother's lifestyle magazines and tried out all their approaches to tidying and storage. I bought boxes and other storage goods and even made my own. But the places I'd tidied so diligently soon reverted to clutter.

After many years of this, I had an epiphany: although my mother had taught me how to cook, do the laundry and clean, no one had ever taught me how to tidy up. Even my mother, who liked housework, wasn't good at tidying.

What were we doing wrong? Frustrated, I stomped around tidying the house with such a scowl on my face that my younger sister dubbed me the Tidying Monster. I was desperate to find the 'right way' to tidy.

How, then, did I find the answer and turn tidying into my profession? It all started with an unusual experience I had the summer I was seventeen.

Soon after my seventeenth birthday, my grandmother, who lived in Kyushu, called me on the phone. 'Hi, Miko,' she said. 'Are you still tidying?'

'Uh-huh. Today I tidied Dad's closet. There were lots of clothes he hasn't worn for years. I'm dying to throw them out,' I confided.

'You haven't changed, have you, Miko?' I heard the sound of her laughter, like little bells tinkling, through the receiver. 'Your father was never able to throw things away, you know. I used to move them without telling him too. Don't worry. I'm sure he'll never notice.'

I loved Grandma Mikako. She was elegant, beautiful and always kind, plus a good cook and seamstress, too. My grandfather, who was a doctor, had died before I was six. Ever since, Grandma Mikako had lived alone in their big European-style house nestled in the woods out in the country. Even though she lived by herself, she still did the housework meticulously, keeping her home spotless. Her kitchen was full of tasteful cookware, and her garden was planted with flowers and herbs that bloomed in different seasons.

She could always tell what I was feeling, and whenever we met, I would confide in her any worries I had about my friends or my studies. I liked to think of her as my Grandma Witch, because she seemed so wise and magical.

'Things are starting to pile up in my house, Miko. Won't you come and tidy it for me? I've left your room just the way it was last time you came. Come and stay with me.'

It had been four years since I'd been there. When I was a child, our family had gone to Kyushu to stay with her every summer. She'd designated the attic room on the second floor as my bedroom. I recalled how the bright morning sunlight poured through the cobalt-blue frame of the square window and felt a thrill of excitement. I could see Grandma and tidy! I consulted my parents immediately, and they agreed to this tidying adventure.

Summer vacation started the following week, and I set off on my first-ever solo trip. It took four and a half hours by plane, train and bus. I got off at the bus stop near my grandmother's house and followed a road along the river through the woods. After about fifteen minutes, a white, square, box-like house with a peaked roof tiled in cobalt blue came into view. My grandmother's house in the forest.

It was just the same as I remembered. Colourful flowers waved in the big garden, which was bordered by a white fence, and a multitude of herbs exuded their fragrance. When I opened the large wooden door to the house, there was my grandmother. She wore an orange scarf and seemed to be waiting for me as if she'd known I was about to arrive. Maybe she was a witch after all.

'Welcome,' she said with a smile. There were tears in her eyes, perhaps from relief. After she'd invited me,

The Chatty Little Box

my father said she'd been terribly worried about me travelling so far alone.

'I love you so much, Grandma.' The words leapt from my mouth before I even said 'Hello'.

'Well, I love you too, dear. You must be tired from the journey. Let's have some tea.'

She led me into the dining room. A Persian rug was spread across the floor under the well-used wooden dining table and chairs. Antique cups and saucers were arranged in the dish cupboard. Grandma loved collecting antique English, German and Scandinavian dishes.

'I'll have the tea ready in a minute. Just wait here,' she said. She took out a set of Danish teacups and a teapot and went into the kitchen.

Even when I was a child, my grandmother had always used her expensive antique dishes when we visited. 'I like using precious things when we're together,' she would say, showering us with warm hospitality.

The sight of those teacups brought back an old memory. Once, I broke one of her cherished cups.

The Chatty Little Box

She'd given us cookies with our tea, and they were so good that I wanted more. Greedily, I reached across to take one from my mother's plate. But my hand knocked  her cup onto the floor. My father, who knew the value of those cups, stared aghast at the broken fragments, and my mother scolded me in dismay.

Grandma quickly swept up the broken pieces at my feet. 'Miko,' she said. 'Are you okay? You didn't cut yourself, did you?' Then she wrapped me in her arms. Shocked by the terrible thing I'd done, I began to sob. While the tears flowed down my face, Grandma stroked my head and whispered in my ear. 'It's all right, Miko. The purpose of that cup was to give me a chance to hug you. Now, its job is done. It's broken, and that's okay. Let's say goodbye to it properly.'

Everything we welcome into our life and all the things we part with have a purpose. Little by little, they change our lives. I learned this fundamental view of the material world from my kind and gentle Grandma Witch.

The smell of peppermint brought me back to the present. Steam rose from the cup in front of me, bearing with it the invigorating aroma. I brought it to my lips and took a sip of the light green liquid. The fatigue of the journey melted away.

'It's delicious.'

'Good. I picked the mint from the garden this morning.'

'It's so relaxing. Your magic is still alive and well, isn't it?'

Grandma laughed. 'It's just tea, Miko,' she said.

'Why did you want me to come and tidy?' I asked. 'You're a genius at tidying yourself.'

'There's something I want you to find.'

'Really? What?'

'A painting your grandfather made a long time ago. It's a small one, about the size of a pocketbook, in a plain wooden frame. I put it away somewhere, but I've searched all over and can't find it.'

I know it's there somewhere, but I just can't find it.

These are words I hear often when helping others tidy up. A favourite hat, a precious necklace, a much-loved book. 'Did it just walk out the door and leave?' my

The Chatty Little Box

clients say in frustration. 'Did a thief or a little elf come and take it? It must be in the house somewhere, but I can't find it for the life of me.'

Tidying up solves this kind of problem quickly. I've seen many clients overjoyed to realise the thing they'd thought was lost was there all along. In that sense, tidying up is like a treasure hunt.

I was thrilled by Grandma's request to help with her treasure hunt. 'All right! I'm sure I can find it once I start tidying. Leave it to me!'

I finished my tea and got to work.

Once I began, however, I realised that tidying was futile. The living room, dining room and kitchen on the first floor, as well as Grandma's bedroom, study and storage closet on the second floor, were all neatly organised. There was nothing left to tidy. That's so like Grandma, I thought, impressed. I looked under the bed and peeked behind the bookcases, but there was no framed painting to be found.

Despondent, I climbed the ladder to my room under the eaves. Poking my head through the trapdoor,

I smelled sunshine. Sunlight was pouring through the square window onto the bed and the white closet. My old summer vacation room. Toys and picture books were placed haphazardly in the bookcase. I climbed the rest of the ladder and stepped into the room. Sensing something behind me, I turned and saw countless boxes of all shapes, sizes and colours stacked against the wall.

Mustard yellow, sky blue, brown and moss green. Salmon-pink stripes and black-and-white checks. Small boxes that fit in the palm. Big boxes tall enough for a child to fit inside. I felt as if I'd slipped back in time. That mosaic of boxes was just the way I remembered.

When I was little, I loved boxes. Cookie boxes, shoe boxes, toy boxes, fruit boxes, boxes that had contained birthday, Christmas, year-end and mid-year gifts. Whenever a box arrived at our house, I would insist on having it. At my grandmother's house, too, I gathered together all the boxes that were there and any new ones that arrived and took them to my attic room.

I still loved boxes and often used them for tidying, but I no longer fanatically collected them the way I did then. Grandma must have remembered how much I loved those boxes and left them just as they were. I felt

a pang of guilt. 'Looks like it's this room that actually needs tidying,' I said to myself. I tightened my red neckerchief (yes, even then I loved wearing a red scarf) and began tidying the attic.

I opened the closet and took out all the clothes. Small garments emerged one after the other. I guessed that my grandmother couldn't bring herself to throw away my childhood clothes. I had no such compunction, however, and placed those that had fulfilled their purpose in the discard pile.

Next, I started on the bookshelves. Grandma had bought me many picture books. These I kept, because good picture books speak to the heart regardless of one's age. I moved on to the toys, which were covered in dust. With a feeling of gratitude and a pang of regret, I put them in the pile of things I was letting go.

Finally, I turned to the enormous stack of boxes. I sighed. Why did I collect so many? They would have to go. I opened each one to check the contents, before putting it on the discard pile. As I did so, the boxes talked to me.

Hurry! Eat me! I'm delicious!
Wear me! I'm still brand new!

The Chatty Little Box

Play with me! Play with me!
I wonder if I'll make her happy?
If you don't eat me soon, I'm going to spoil!

The boxes had been guarding my memories all this time, so opening them was like meeting my childhood self. Tidying, I thought, is like a journey through time.

Hold on there! Don't get caught up in those memories, I chided myself. After all, you've got to throw them all away. I sank into a trance, opening one after another non-stop and muttering things like, 'This one's old. I'll never use that one. This one's dirty. Argh, I don't need any of them!'

I reached for a box that had previously been hidden deep inside the stack. It had white and cobalt-blue stripes, the same colour as the roof, and was topped with a yellow-edged lid. Opening it, I saw a small painting in a wooden frame. It was of a little girl in a white dress holding a box with blue stripes. An image flashed into my mind – my grandfather, brush in hand, gazing at me as he painted. The girl in the picture was me.

133

In a box of a house was an equally box-like room; in that box room was a little striped box; in the little striped box was a picture; and in that picture was me, clutching a little striped box. That image of me, projected in layers on my brain, spun round and round, making me dizzy. I felt as if I'd wandered into a maze of endless corridors. There was a snap, like a light being switched off, and I lost consciousness.

I woke to the sound of a sulky little boy's voice. *Hey! Wake up! How long are you going to sleep? Wake up, I said!*

I looked around but couldn't see anyone. How long had I been lying on the floor? Outside, it was already dark, and the light of the moon now shone faintly into the room.

It's about time! You were always like that, Miko, even as a kid. Once you fell asleep, you wouldn't wake up.

I thought I must be hearing things, but the voice was definitely coming from inside the room. I peered towards the sound.

Over here, Tidying Monster. The yellow-bordered lid on the box with cobalt-blue stripes was flapping as it talked. My mouth dropped open and I screamed. Or at least I intended to, but no sound came out. In my

The Chatty Little Box

surprise, I ended up flapping my mouth open and shut just like the box's lid.

You've really become a kind of monster, you know. The box frowned, or rather, its stripes squidged together. *You see all things as enemies and hate them.*

'Who are you?' I finally managed to squeak.

Talk about insulting. You've forgotten me even though you used to play with me all the time? I'm Hako!

I stared at him, mirroring his frown. On closer inspection, I realised he was a cookie box that I'd loved as a child. Timidly, I began conversing with the sarcastic box. 'I hate them?'

That's right. Before you fell asleep, you were saying, 'I've got to throw this away. I've got to throw that away,' and being so unkind. You were tidying this room as if you hated doing it. Even though you used to love tidying when you were little.

'I used to enjoy it that much, did I?' He was right. Tidying was no longer any fun. Instead, it had become painful. Without even realising it, I'd started hating the things and spaces I tidied and was just looking for things to chuck.

You're fixated on what to throw away, but that's not what counts. It's finding what sparks joy. Right?

'What sparks joy ...' I was at a loss for words. The box had argued me down, making me acutely aware that my approach had been all wrong. Until then, my sole focus had been on reducing the volume of things and finding good storage solutions. That's why, no matter how hard I tried, nothing I tidied ever stayed tidied, and I ended up hating things – when in reality, tidying is the ability to recognise what brings joy and makes life richer and more fun.

'Miko! Suppertime!' Grandma called, and the scent of curry wafted into the room.

'Coming,' I replied and headed for the ladder.

Hey! Miko! Did you hear what I said? Hako toddled after me. If Grandma saw that box talking, she'd fall over in surprise. I picked him up and shut his lid, then climbed down the ladder.

On white antique plates, my grandmother had placed a mound of rice topped with aubergine, tomato and courgette, all picked from her garden and deep-fried without batter. Over this, she poured curry made with her own original spices.

The Chatty Little Box

'I'm starving!' I said as the complex bouquet of spices teased my nostrils.

Please have some, my plate said to me, sounding like an elegant elderly lady.

I'm sure you'll find it delicious, said the well-polished silver spoon in the voice of an elderly gentleman.

It seemed that, in addition to boxes, I could now hear dishes. Grandma didn't seem to hear a thing, which meant that she couldn't hear Hako either.

'It looks fabulous!' Gingerly, I picked up the talking spoon and popped some curry into my mouth. The thick sauce mingled with the flavours of the summer vegetables. 'Delicious,' I sighed.

'I'm glad you like it,' Grandma said with a smile.

I had put the painting of the little girl holding a box on a chair. Grandma caught sight of it and smiled. 'Just as I thought. You found it, Miko,' she murmured.

'The only reason you couldn't find it was that you were reluctant to tidy my room, right?'

'No, I actually tidied up the attic several times, but for some reason, I couldn't find this painting. Or that box,' she said, looking at Hako perched on my lap. 'I haven't seen that one for a long time.'

'Really?'

'Yes. I wonder where it was hiding.' She laughed in a knowing way. Hako jerked, and I hastily placed my hand on him.

'You've loved using boxes to tidy things from the time your grandfather made that painting,' she said with a faraway look in her eyes.

'I liked tidying and boxes that long ago?'

'You sure did.'

'Today I realised that tidying, which I used to love, had become a chore.'

Grandma just listened with her eyes on my face. I was sure that she could read my mind. 'But I think this box can teach me how to enjoy tidying again,' I finished, hugging him tightly. *Hey! Cut that out!* he said, squirming as though embarrassed.

'He's your buddy, isn't he?'

'My buddy?'

'You know, Miko, I think someday you two will make tidying your profession.' Shifting her gaze to the box, my Grandma Witch giggled like a mischievous little girl.

A few years later, my grandmother's prediction came true. I never dreamed that one day I would make tidying

my job. But a friend who'd heard about my peculiar habit asked me to help her tidy up. Then her friend asked me to help too, and like beads slipped on a string, one thing led to another. Before I knew it, tidying had become my profession.

Mind you, I certainly never expected I'd end up being able to hear everything talk or that I'd have a sassy little box tagging along to all my jobs.

Quite shamelessly, Hako is always sure to remind me, 'Don't forget, your grandma said I'm your buddy.'

Whatever. I'm enjoying each lively day I spend with my sidekick as we meet other chatty things.

Grandma still lives alone in the white box in the forest. And in the box-like room in the attic of that box in the forest are the boxes that even now spark joy for me.

ROOM 6
The Hoarder's Noisy Trash

Michiya Kise (age 52)

Three bicycles lay collapsed in a pile on the porch of the old two-storey house. Their tyres were flat, and the frames were rusted. I squeezed past them and pressed the intercom button.

'Please come inside,' came a deep, indistinct voice. I opened the door. Even before I crossed the threshold, the stench of rubbish assaulted my nose, and angry voices rushed into my ears.

Put me on! Put me on!

If you're going to treat me like this, why don't you just throw me away?

Let me out! I wanna get out of here!

I looked down. Shoes, shoes and more shoes were piled randomly in the entranceway. Trainers and sandals, leather shoes and boots. Screams rose from the bottom as if being reeled up on a spider thread dangled into the depths of hell by a ghoul.

I'm dying of thirst ...

I can't breathe. Hurry up and open me!

Rain ... Is it raining yet?

Like travellers lost in the desert, umbrellas gasped with thirst. Many were crammed into an umbrella stand beside the entrance, while clear plastic umbrellas and children's umbrellas that couldn't fit in the stand leaned against the wall around it. There must have been at least fifty. Their ribs were deep red with rust, showing how long they'd been abandoned.

Read me ... Read me ... Read me ...

Strained voices came from stacks of newspapers and magazines piled high inside the door. In the hallway beyond them were a faded suitcase, pieces of ripped cardboard and clothing cases filled with all kinds of things. Every gap had been stuffed with something: bulging plastic and paper bags, their contents unrecognisable; giveaway cushions with unknown cartoon characters; vinyl handbags; and souvenirs of all sorts, from carved wooden bears to key holders, from traditional *kokeshi* dolls to snow domes. All of them groaned and wailed.

It's like a haunted house, not a hoarder's house. Hako's voice shook as he peeked fearfully through the lid.

The Hoarder's Noisy Trash

'Don't say things like that. He's our client.' I snapped the lid shut and looked around. 'He must have been in a lot of pain to let it get like this.'

I was flustered. The house's condition far exceeded my imagination. I'm used to cluttered homes because most people who need help tidying haven't been able to do it on their own. But never had I seen this much stuff.

I managed to get the door open, but couldn't see how we were going to get through the jumble of things jamming the entrance and hallway. As I stood frozen on the doorstep, I heard the voice again. 'Please come in. Keep your shoes on.'

Hako and I looked at each other. Two cats, one black and one white, emerged from the mass of stuff and led us down the hallway into the house. Although opposite in colour, their shape and gait made them look like identical twins.

'Sorry,' I gasped as I scrambled over the mountain of shoes and pushed my way through the stacks of newspaper bundles.

The cats led us to the back of the house, which was just as cluttered. Several mattresses leaned against the window, shutting out the light. Heaps of things rose up from the floor like giant anthills. I assumed this was the kitchen and dining area because I glimpsed two fridges, two dining tables and four microwaves poking through the junk.

'Over here.' For the third time, I heard the man's voice. It was coming from deep within what looked like an overgrown jungle of stuff. The two cats slipped through the gaps, leading the way, and I ploughed after them in search of the man. All the while, I was assailed by pleading voices.

Help!

Get me out of here!

The smells of man, beast, mould and dust mingled into an odour I couldn't believe belonged in this world.

Hako covered his nose, or really his ribbon holes, with his ribbon. *Now that's what I call pandemonium! It's scary...*

He was right. The clamour sounded like a chorus of inmates from Hell. I was reminded of *tsukumogami* from Japanese folklore; old tools and household items that have come alive.

The Hoarder's Noisy Trash

I sighed. 'You're usually so cocky,' I said. 'How can you be such a coward at a time like this?' Squeezing between two dish cabinets, I forced my way into a space that had probably been the living room. Arranged in a U-shape around a large TV screen were three mismatched sofas. On the middle one sat a large man dressed in a yellow sweatsuit and clutching a game controller. The two cats, who had reached this room before me, sat primly on the sofas to either side, their faces turned my way. They looked just like *komainu*, the dog statues that guard either side of the gate to a Shinto shrine.

The man's wavy hair was uncombed, and he was engrossed in a video game, his fingers moving quickly over the controls. Colourful puzzle pieces appeared on the screen; he positioned them into the right slots to make a pattern. Obviously new, the black TV gleamed, standing out among the drab sofas, dressers and obsolete TV screens that surrounded it.

'Are you ... Michiya Kise?' I asked.

'That's right. Just a moment,' he answered without taking his eyes off the screen as he pressed the buttons on the controller in quick succession.

Play with me! Play with me!

Couldn't you at least turn my switch on sometimes?
No, not yours! Mine! I'm next!

All kinds of game consoles, from old to new, lay scattered at his feet. They twittered like a flock of fairies clamouring for attention. Electrical wires connecting them to the TV crawled across the floor like a tangle of vines, as though tethering the man to the sofa.

'Thanks for coming.'

At the sound of his voice, I raised my eyes from the cluttered floor. The puzzle pieces that had appeared in the middle of the screen formed a straight line and vanished. The two cats opened their mouths and mewed in unison, as if praising his skill. 'I bet you were

The Hoarder's Noisy Trash

surprised to see such a mess,' he said, looking at me for the first time.

Go ahead. Tell him it looks like a haunted house, Hako said irritably.

I shut his lid. 'Frankly, I was a little surprised,' I said. 'But the fact that you hired me means you want to tidy up, right?'

'Well ... I'm not sure about that,' he said. 'The neighbours started complaining, so I thought I'd better do something, but ...'

'How did it get like this?'

His gaze wandered back to the screen. 'I don't know. By the time I realised it, it was already this way.' His dull, lifeless eyes returned to my face. Of course, he couldn't hear the clamouring voices of the things that filled his house.

No matter the home, clutter doesn't happen by itself. The person living in it does the cluttering. And of those who clutter, there are just three types. People who can't throw things away. People who can't put things away. And people who can't throw or put things away. He appeared to be the latter type. Moreover, he was a very severe case. I usually start by asking my clients to imagine their ideal lifestyle, then have them sort their items by category. Starting with their clothes, they touch each item; they choose those that spark joy and let go of those that don't. But when there is too much stuff, it's difficult to know where to begin, let alone to tell what sparks joy. In these rare cases, there's only one thing to do.

Better start chucking things from one end of this house to the other, Hako said, voicing my thoughts.

We had no choice. I turned back to Mr Kise. 'It looks like there's a lot you could let go of,' I said.

He cocked his head to one side and shrugged, sinking his neck into his large frame as if he didn't agree. 'You think so, do you?' he said, addressing his remarks to the black cat. 'I suppose to other people this looks like a pile of rubbish, but to me, all these things have meaning. It seems kind of fanatical to tell people to throw away what they don't need or to live with the bare minimum. I don't agree with that.'

I often get comments like this from my clients. Although they hire me to help them tidy up, some insist that even if their place looks like a garbage heap, it's really a treasure trove.

'What matters, Mr Kise, is not how much you

have, but whether you know what you have and where everything is,' I said.

'Oh, well, in that case, I've got a pretty good idea,' he said.

'All right then. What things in your house spark joy?' I asked.

Mr Kise shifted his gaze from the black cat to the white. 'Joy,' he murmured. 'I've never thought about that.'

When I ask people who can't throw things away this question, it's clear that most of them have never really looked at what brings them happiness. If we don't know what we need or want, we keep collecting things until we're buried in stuff. It's only when we feel gratitude for each item we have that the space we live in becomes our own. If all the things in Mr Kise's house had been properly loved and appreciated, they wouldn't have become such desperate, tortured souls.

Knowing that he would need a push to get started, I decided to be blunt. 'If you throw away everything that doesn't spark joy for you, I'm sure you won't regret it one bit. None of my clients has ever complained about wanting back something they threw away.'

He gave a wry smile, perhaps taken aback by my confidence. 'I won't regret it one bit, huh? That's a pretty radical claim.'

He's right, Miko! You're always so extreme. What makes you so sure – Oh-oh ...

The cats were staring at Hako. Could they hear him? I hastily shut his lid and continued. 'Once you experience the fact that you can live without all this stuff, your life will become much easier. You can switch from searching for things to focusing on what you really want to do.'

Mr Kise flushed a dark red and rose from the couch. 'If I could do something about this, it would never have happened!' His body, round as a full moon, bumped

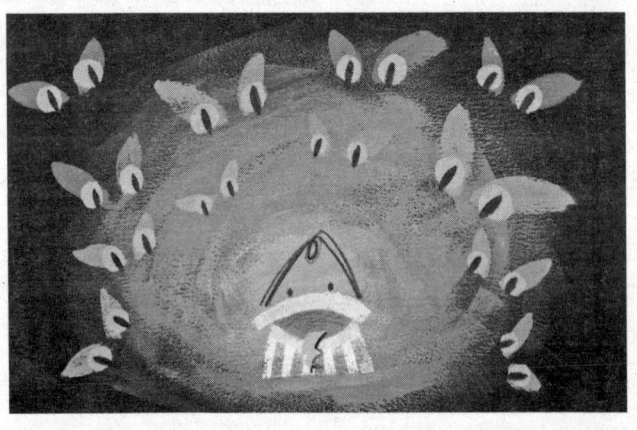

The Hoarder's Noisy Trash

into things and sent them flying. The two cats shrieked, perhaps fearing for his safety. Instantly, cats appeared from everywhere, like reinforcements coming to the rescue. Soon the space around the sofas was filled with twelve of them. Where had they been hiding?

They turned towards me, hissing and yowling as if to protect their master, and their eyes gleamed menacingly. Some of them noticed Hako and began scratching at his lid.

Stop that! This place is driving me nuts! Talking things, howling cats! Just stop! Hako scuttled away, slipping through the gaps to escape.

'Quiet!' shouted Mr Kise. He scooped up the black cat and the white cat, tucking one in the crook of each arm. The yowling ceased. 'Sorry to startle you,' he said. 'They were just trying to protect me because I was upset by what you said.'

Twelve pairs of eyes stared at me as if trying to judge whether I was friend or foe. Mr Kise's eyes softened, and he began introducing them. He'd named them after the Japanese names for the months, and he went in order from January to December.

'This black cat here is Mutsuki, and the white one is

Kisaragi. That calico over there is Yayoi, and the tabby cat beside it is Uzuki. The one with the bobbed tail is Satsuki and the fluffy one is Minazuki. The three cats playing over there with the marbled black, white and grey fur are siblings. From the left, they're Fumizuki, Hazuki and Nagatsuki. Or maybe they're Hazuki, Nagatsuki and Fumizuki. Hmm. Oh well, they're siblings at any rate ... The one over there with the round ears is Kannazuki, and this grey beauty here is Shimotsuki. And last of all, the kitten who joined us recently is Shiwasu.'

I couldn't help smiling. 'Your house may be disorganised but you've kept all your cats in order by naming them after the months,' I chuckled.

'That's true. My stuff is all over the place, but the cats are properly organised.' He laughed, making his round face look even rounder. 'I never thought I would end up taking in so many cats. I just got so lonely living by myself, that's all. I can't take in any more though, because I've used up all the months of the year.'

Hako was still frantically evading the three cat siblings who wanted to play with him, but he paused to say, *Ha. I bet you'll name the next ones after the days of the month until you have thirty-one. Before that happens, you better tidy up.*

As if he'd heard Hako, Mr Kise surveyed the room slowly. 'I think I'll give it a try,' he said.

'Really?'

'Yes, but I'm afraid.'

'Afraid?'

'That I might throw away something I shouldn't.'

I'm afraid to throw things away. I often hear this from people whose rooms or desks are covered in clutter. They have so much it's probably hard for them to judge which things are valuable and which ones aren't.

What would be the best way to help Mr Kise let go of things? I wondered. An idea popped into my head, and I yanked off Hako's lid, ignoring his protests that I should treat him with more respect. From inside, I pulled out a white Polaroid camera.

'A camera?' said Mr Kise with a mystified look.

'Yes. If you think an item is one you could discard, take a photo of it,' I said.

'A photo?'

'For some reason, taking a photo seems to help us let things go. Perhaps the memories and feelings connected with that item are transferred to the photo. Would you like to try it?'

The Hoarder's Noisy Trash

Mr Kise took the camera and began walking through the jungle of stuff. He paused to touch an old TV he no longer used. After thinking for a moment, he pressed the camera's shutter.

One by one, things began to emerge from the mounds. A tangle of electrical cords of unknown purpose, leftover prescription medicine, batteries that were no longer identifiable as used or new, bundles of business cards and New Year's cards bound with rubber bands, old protective charms, spare buttons, mobile phones dating back through several eras of technology, manuals for household appliances, boxes of masks and bottles of disinfectant bought in bulk. As these things appeared, I tried to encourage Mr Kise by sharing advice.

'Unidentified electrical cords will remain unknown forever, so let's throw them away. You'll never use spare buttons. If you love something and wear it long enough for a button to come off, it's almost always a sign that it's reached the end of its life. Get rid of appliance manuals right away. You can find all the information in them through a quick search online. In general, paper stuff like business cards and New Year's cards should be discarded unless it's something particularly important.

Miscellaneous items and documents that are kept "just because", pile up "just because". From these, choose only those that spark joy.'

Mr Kise spent the next few weeks taking photos and discarding. It was almost as if he'd shed some evil spirit that had made him hoard. Strangely enough, his things, so anguished by neglect that they had resembled *tsukumogami*, sighed with relief when he finally let them go. The cats guided him back and forth through the jungle of stuff and mewed in encouragement each time he decided to discard. They seemed more attuned to what did and didn't spark joy for him than he was. With their support, he was able to part with almost all the stuff that had been piled in heaps in the living room, the dining room and the kitchen.

'Once you've chosen what to keep,' I told him, 'the next step is to decide where to keep those things and then store them by category, such as stationery supplies, medicine, and so on. Things of similar nature or shape get along well, so they feel more settled when stored near each other. It's a lot like playing a word association

The Hoarder's Noisy Trash

game. For example, PC-related goods can be stored beside electrical cords or other things that feel electrical. If you approach it like this, you'll find that similar things naturally end up side by side. Oh, and you're bound to come across small change. When you do, put it in your wallet. If you have any piggy banks, exchange the coins inside for bills at the bank.'

Once he'd finished storing everything in the living room and the dining and kitchen area, Mr Kise moved on to the hallway and front entrance. He decided to discard the stacks of newspapers and cardboard, as well as almost all the umbrellas and shoes at the front door. Next, he tackled the books that had been stacked like some intricate puzzle game on the stairs to the second floor. Despite interference from the kitten Shiwasu, who wanted to play, he finally reached the second floor and started on the bedroom. As we entered, I heard voices arguing heatedly near the bed.

Hot! Hot! Hot!

Cold! Cold! Cold!

I peered in the direction of the noise. A heater and an electric fan were arguing amid a heap of bedding and furniture.

I opened the closet. Immediately, Christmas and New Year's ornaments and Halloween pumpkin decorations, which were all tucked away under the clothes, began competing for attention.

Merry Christmas!

Happy New Year!

Trick or treat!

What a mixed-up sense of season, Hako remarked with a laugh.

Beside him I carried on advising Mr Kise. 'As you continue selecting what you want to keep, you'll reach a point where you know the volume of things that works for you. Once you get there, you can avoid returning to clutter by designating a specific place to store each item, because clutter is caused by not being able to put things back where they belong.'

Mr Kise continued to snap photos of different items and discard them. As the volume of stuff decreased, light began to fill the room and fresh air flowed through. The twelve cats sprawled out in the sunshine to enjoy the breeze, purring contentedly.

The last room was the child's room at the far end of the corridor on the second floor. There was a small bed, a desk and a bookcase filled with a disorganised collection of picture books and manga. The walls were covered in drawings, paintings and calligraphy drills, all clearly done by a child. But the room was silent. As I looked inside, I knew that everything had to be treated with care.

From behind me Mr Kise said, 'I got divorced ten years ago when my son was still in elementary school. My wife left and took him with her.'

He stepped into the room and placed his hand on a play tent with toy robots and stuffed dinosaurs inside. Cars and trains left about the floor wore a thick layer of dust. Everything seemed to have turned to stone. The black cat and the white cat padded across the floor, leaving paw prints in the grey dust.

'I worked for a video game company and was always on the job. Late nights. Never took any holidays. Even when I was at home, I didn't talk to my family much. Whenever they tried to talk to me, I'd say I was busy. But "busy" is a dangerous word. It cuts off all conversation with other people and yourself. It makes you believe there's no need to look at what really matters.'

The Hoarder's Noisy Trash

Mr Kise muttered these words as he crouched to open a cardboard box at the foot of the desk. Inside it were a portrait with the words, 'Thanks Dad', shoulder massage tickets made from origami paper, medals won at school sports events, report cards, and a photo of a boy and his parents at a school entrance ceremony.

'We got along in those days. I wonder what happened … I was busy, busy, busy. Working flat out to support my family. But then my wife just got up and left. I begged her to stay, but she said she'd reached her limit long ago.'

He rose and walked over to the two cats. They were staring at the white closet doors. Mr Kise followed their gaze.

'Once I was left on my own, I felt like a switch had been flipped off inside me. I quit my job two years later and holed up in the house. I worked temporary remote jobs to make ends meet. I felt so lonely, I couldn't bring myself to throw any of my family's stuff away. And I started buying things aimlessly online. Before I realised it, my house had become the way you saw it.'

Our living space is a reflection of our inner state. The things in that space are there because, at some point, we ourselves chose to keep them. To turn a blind eye to the things we own is akin to turning our back on life. By facing everything we've held on to, along with the memories and feelings connected with them, we can begin to understand ourselves.

Over the final few weeks, Mr Kise had continued to face his inner self. Now he'd come to the last portal. What lay behind those white doors? Hako and I held our breath, waiting.

Mr Kise inhaled deeply, then grasped the handles on the double doors and pulled. They squeaked as they swung open revealing an astonishing array of time pieces, all crammed in haphazardly. Wall clocks, alarm clocks and wristwatches, as well as more unusual cuckoo clocks and pocket watches. Not a sound could be heard from any of them.

'They've stopped working.' Mr Kise's voice broke the silence like a drop of water falling into a pond. None of the clocks were ticking. It was as if time had been stopped and shoved into the closet. Mr Kise stood frozen, just like the clocks.

'There are just two reasons why we can't let go of things,' I said. 'Attachment to the past or anxiety about

The Hoarder's Noisy Trash

the future. And there are only three choices we can make about the things in our lives. Face them now, face them sometime in the future or ignore them until we die. I recommend facing them now so that time can move forward. Our space should be dedicated to the person we are becoming, not to who we were in the past.'

With trembling hands, Mr Kise reached out and touched one clock after another, recalling the time he'd spent with his family, memories which he had locked away.

'I finally get it,' he murmured. 'I was scared. Afraid that if I threw away the things in this house, I would lose all my memories. Memories of life with my wife and son. I was afraid to lose my own past.'

He reached into the back of the closet and pulled out a child's alarm clock with a cat painted on it. The two cats, one black, one white, meowed when they saw it, as if recognising it. At that moment, the second hand began to move, and I heard a ticking sound. In that space where time stood still, the cat clock was the only clock counting time.

Hako glanced up at me with a smile. *It's as if it has a soul of its own. Do you think it's a* tsukumogami?

I often run into mysterious phenomena like this when tidying up. It's not at all unusual.

At that moment, Mr Kise's phone rang, and he drew it from his pocket. He raised his eyebrows when he saw the name of the caller on the screen.

'Who is it?' I asked.

'My son,' he said in a small voice. 'Why is he calling me out of the blue?'

As he stood there hesitating, Hako and I looked at each other. We knew that one mysterious occurrence often causes a chain reaction.

'Mr Kise, answer the phone,' I urged him.

'But ... I don't know what to say.'

'You'll be fine. While tidying up, you've found lots

of things you can talk with him about. The robot toy, the stuffed dinosaurs, the portrait he drew of you, the massage tickets, the sports medals, the cat clock. These are all memories of your son.'

'That's true.' His finger shaking, he tapped his phone and answered timidly, 'Kenta? How're you doing? Yeah, I'm fine. Uh-huh. Sure. Let's meet up. It's been a long time. Great. I'll see you here on Sunday then. Actually, I've been tidying up this place. Oh, and I found your clock. The one I bought you for your birthday. The alarm clock with the cat on it. Yeah, it's still working.'

While he was talking, the other ten cats trickled into the room. They all watched him supportively as he continued the halting conversation with his son.

ROOM 7
Storytelling Photo Albums

Chiyo Aoyama (age 83)

After my fifteen-minute climb up the hill from the station, a house with an ultramarine roof came into view. I had been commuting to this house for seven days. Its owner, Chiyo Aoyama, would soon be eighty-four.

'This will be my last tidy-up,' she'd told me. 'I want to take it slowly.'

I'm so tired of climbing this hill every day, Hako grumbled under my arm.

'But you aren't even doing the walking!' I retorted.

I know, but I still get tired.

'What's your problem? Anyway, it's our last day, so you won't need to come anymore.'

Oh. Well then. I'll miss this scenery.

'Make up your mind,' I said in exasperation, but Hako was staring back absently at the road we'd climbed. I followed his gaze. At the bottom of the hill, the sea was

Storytelling Photo Albums

sparkling in the summer light. It was the same bright blue as the roof of the house.

Chiyo greeted me at the front door. 'Hi, Miko. Thanks for coming to help me finish tidying up.' She was wearing a royal-blue dress, one she'd found at the back of her closet while we were tidying. She'd considered it so precious she almost never wore it. When I heard that, I urged her to put it on. 'Things that spark joy should be worn anywhere, anytime, even in the house.'

'That dress looks great on you,' I said now, giving her a big smile.

'Thank you,' she said, returning my smile. 'I feel so happy when I wear it.' She led me through the living room, which had already been neatly tidied, to a room in the back of the house. I'm quite petite but she was even smaller than me. She looked like a little fairy as she flitted across the floor in her royal-blue dress.

The room we came to wasn't very large. It had once been the children's room, but was now used for storage. The built-in bookshelves were filled with photo albums that numbered at least a hundred. Some were as thick as dictionaries, while others were thin paper albums given away by photo shops, or tall albums that resembled

photo catalogues. On the top bunk of the children's bunkbed were plastic bags and cookie tins stuffed with countless photos that had never made it into an album. More photos overflowed from cardboard boxes on the floor. This was the last room, our last tidying task.

I tightened my red neckerchief and got ready to work.

The correct order for tidying is to start with clothes and work your way through books, papers, *komono* (miscellaneous items), and sentimental things. Photographs should be left to the very end. I always make sure my clients follow this order.

'When I asked for your help, it was because I wanted to do something about these photos,' Chiyo said. 'I was quite surprised when you told me I wasn't at the stage where I could work on them yet.'

'Sorry to have kept you waiting.'

'Why do you save them for last?' she asked, gazing around at the photo-filled room.

'There's a good reason for that order,' I explained while sorting through some of the photos on the floor. 'We start with things that are easier to let go of, like clothes. This lets us build our own pace as we work towards things we have a stronger attachment to.'

'I see. So that's why you leave sentimental items to the end.'

'That's right. And of all the sentimental things, photos are the hardest to part with. They're so strongly associated with the owner's memories that they seem like the memories themselves. This makes them very hard to let go of. If we try to sort through them first, before we've developed our ability to judge what sparks joy when we touch it, we'll get stuck, and tidying will come to a standstill.'

'I wonder if I'm really ready.' She looked anxiously inside a box filled with photos.

'I'm sure you are,' I said confidently. 'Look how far you've come in the last six days. That means you can already tell quite accurately what sparks joy for you. Approach it as if you were tackling the summit of tidying.' As I shared these encouraging words, I reached out and picked up a round tin that had once contained *gaufre* buttercream wafers.

'I hope you're right,' she said.

'There's one other reason I leave photos to the last.

Did you notice how many you found as you were tidying other places?'

'Yes, lots. In books and desk drawers and envelopes.'

'Often, they turn up still in the envelope they came in when they were developed. Photos seem to appear from just about everywhere when tidying. So that's another good reason to leave them to the end.'

The high-pitched chime of the doorbell rang suddenly, as if it had been waiting for me to stop talking.

Yikes! Hako jumped in surprise and stuck out his tongue. I hastily pushed his pink ribbon back under the lid.

'Oh, that must be the children,' Chiyo exclaimed. Smiling, she headed for the front door.

Children? Hako's stripes squished together in a frown. He didn't like kids or pets, as both tended to notice he was no ordinary box.

Chiyo returned leading a man and a woman who looked around the same age as my parents. Hako breathed a sigh of relief. *I suppose it makes sense they'd be that old*, he said.

'Miko, let me introduce you,' said Chiyo. 'This is my son Shunsuke and my daughter Ikumi.'

Shunsuke and Ikumi bowed in greeting but they didn't smile. Perhaps they weren't used to seeing other people in their childhood home. They were both tall and looked so unlike Chiyo that if she hadn't introduced them as her children, I wouldn't have guessed they were related.

Catching sight of Chiyo's dress, Shunsuke exclaimed, 'Mum, what's got into you? Why are you wearing such nice clothes in the house? Shouldn't you wear something else for tidying?'

'I'm wearing it precisely because I'm tidying. Miko's a pro, and look at the pretty white dress she's wearing. Tidying's a festival, a special send-off for the things I'm letting go, so I want to look my best. Don't you agree, Miko?'

I smiled and nodded. Chiyo's eyes shone with sincerity. In contrast, her two children examined me rather doubtfully.

'It's no big deal, Shunsuke,' Ikumi said. 'If she wants to wear it, why not? But I wonder if it's a good idea to throw everything away. I tried that myself not along ago when it was a fad, but I just ended up collecting more stuff. And as for minimalists, their houses all look identical, which is kind of creepy, don't you think?'

Ooh, that's nasty, Hako said with a scowl. I couldn't help smiling as I recalled how snarky he could be himself.

'Hanging on to things doesn't necessarily mean we appreciate them,' I explained to Ikumi. 'Reducing what we have and keeping only what we really love can reinvigorate our relationship with those things. The goal of my tidying method isn't getting rid of stuff. It's to discover what's precious, what really brings us joy. If you take a look at the rooms your mother has already tidied, I'm sure you'll find they're filled with a quiet charm and only things she loves.'

Shunsuke and Ikumi said nothing. Chiyo broke the silence. 'I asked you to come because I want to tidy up the photos with you.'

Shunsuke looked dubiously at the shelves packed with photo albums. 'You want us to help with the photos? But you've done the rest of the house with her. Why not let the pro finish the job?'

Ikumi, who had been staring aghast at all the photos on the floor, chimed in. 'There's no need to tidy them now, is there? It would be a nice little project for your old age.'

Chiyo's face fell, and she stared at her feet. 'That's not what I mean.'

I jumped in, spurred on by her forlorn expression. 'Many people set aside photos thinking they'll enjoy sorting through them sometime in the future, but sometime never comes. I think we get a greater sense of fulfilment every day if we tidy up our photos and display the ones that spark joy where we can see them.'

'But it doesn't seem right to rush. Won't you feel like you're throwing away your memories along with the photos?' Ikumi seemed intent on changing her mother's mind, as if desperate to avoid what looked like a daunting task.

'Tidying up doesn't mean throwing away the past,' I countered. 'Our identity and what we've experienced in life won't disappear just because we choose to get rid of something. We live in the present. No matter how wonderful the past was, it's meaningless if we aren't putting it to good use here and now.'

'Oh, I just remembered something!' Shunsuke interrupted as if grasping the baton passed on by his sister. 'I've heard there's a service where you can send all your photos and they'll scan them and digitise them for you. Why not try that?'

I pressed on. 'The whole point of tidying up is to make sure our memories nourish our lives now and in the future. When we confront our possessions one by one, they stir up many emotions. Through the process of choosing the ones that spark joy, we can discover for the first time what we really love and want in life.' I spoke passionately because I knew why Chiyo had invited her children to come.

Chiyo's eyes had been fixed on the ground throughout, but now she raised her head and said quietly, 'I wanted to do this with you. So we could share our memories. Is that too much to ask?'

Neither Shunsuke nor Ikumi had any rebuttal for this plea. They looked at each other, then back to her and nodded, seemingly resigned.

Shunsuke reached out to pick up an album. 'Okay then,' he said. 'Where should we start?'

'The first step,' I said, 'is to take all the photos out of any albums, cans, boxes, bags and envelopes. After that, we'll pick them up one by one.'

'That's quite a job!'

'It is, but it's a necessary part of the process. When you physically touch something, you'll be surprised at how clearly you can tell what sparks joy and what doesn't.'

Together, they began removing photos from the albums. As they did so, photos of Chiyo as a little girl, a student and a new employee emerged. She picked up

one of her wedding and gazed at it fondly. There she was in her wedding dress flanked by her husband, a tall man wearing a tuxedo. Shunsuke and Ikumi's resemblance to their father was obvious.

The photo showed Chiyo handing her parents a bouquet. Both Hako and I clearly heard the words, *Mum, Dad, thank you for everything.*

'Look at me,' said Chiyo. 'I was so chubby.'

'Really?' Ikumi stared at the photo. 'Mum, you look really beautiful.'

'I'm so glad you didn't take after me, Ikumi,' Chiyo said with a wry smile.

Shunsuke had come to look over their shoulders at

the photo. 'Dad sure was handsome, wasn't he? Guess I took after him, huh?'

Ikumi rolled her eyes. 'Honestly. You're so vain, Shunsuke.'

'Look at what I found,' he said, ignoring her remark. He showed them the photo he was holding.

I heard a little boy crying. *Mum, it hurts!* It was a family photo taken in front of a kindergarten. Little boy Shunsuke, dressed smartly in a blazer for his entrance ceremony, was crying and his nose was running.

'Why was I crying?'

'You're kidding. You mean you really don't remember?' Ikumi exclaimed.

'No, not at all. What happened?'

'After the ceremony,' said Chiyo, 'you climbed to the top of the jungle gym in the playground and fell off. Luckily, you weren't injured.' As she recalled the incident, she chuckled, and Ikumi's shoulders started to shake too.

'You looked like that in every photo we took that day, because you wouldn't stop crying.' Ikumi laughed. 'I think that might be my first memory. You crying at the entrance ceremony.'

'Wow, talk about not cool,' said Shunsuke, scratching

Storytelling Photo Albums

his head. He turned and opened a cookie tin. As soon as he began removing photos, I heard a voice. *Mum, catch the ball properly!* An older version of the boy Shunsuke stood glaring at the camera, a baseball glove on one hand. Shunsuke stared at his younger self.

'Why do I look so mad in this photo?' he asked.

'We were playing catch,' said Chiyo with a remorseful expression, 'but I was terrible at it and kept fumbling the ball.'

'You were so mean, Shunsuke!' said Ikumi, jumping to their mother's defence. 'You got so mad at Mum. You cried and yelled and generally behaved like a little brat.'

'Now I remember, Mum. I gave you such a hard time that you went out and got yourself a baseball glove to practise with. I'm sorry I was so selfish. I probably just wanted your attention.'

'It doesn't matter, Shunsuke. Besides, I got pretty good at it, you know.'

'Yeah, I remember that too. You practised really hard. Thanks, Mum.' Shunsuke bobbed his head appreciatively.

Ikumi held out a photo she'd found. 'What's this unidentifiable blob I'm holding?' she asked.

The girl in the centre of the photo spoke with a trembling voice. *Mummy, I made you a birthday cake but ...*

Shunsuke peered at the photo. 'It's hard to tell. Is it something you made from paper clay, Ikumi?'

'This?' Chiyo said. 'It's the first birthday cake Ikumi ever made for me!'

'Oh, I remember now!' said Ikumi. 'We couldn't afford to buy a whole birthday cake. I really wanted you to have a big one, so I tried to make one myself instead. But it was a disaster.'

'And you bawled your eyes out,' Shunsuke said teasingly. 'I remember you crying and saying, "It's not working!"'

Storytelling Photo Albums

Chiyo gazed at the photo with a dreamy look in her eyes and ran her finger over the little girl's face. 'You made me so happy,' she said.

Ikumi looked at the failed cake in the photo and laughed. 'In the end,' she said, 'we all went to the cake shop near the station and bought four pieces of strawberry shortcake. I'll never forget how delicious that was. There's nothing like a cake made by a proper patissier.'

Scenes like this are common when people tidy their photos together. What one person has forgotten another will remember clearly. Families support one another by complementing each other's memories and emotions in this way.

'Your cake, Ikumi,' Chiyo murmured. 'It was delicious.' Then, as though suddenly returning to the present, she stood up. 'You must be tired,' she said. 'I'll go make some tea. Wait here for a little bit.' She left the room.

'I'll give you a hand,' I said, following Chiyo into the kitchen.

'Discarding photos is hard, isn't it?' said Chiyo, as she put the kettle on to boil. 'There are lots that don't spark joy, but I'm not sure I can bring myself to throw them away. Even though I was feeling pretty confident after six days of tidying.'

I nodded. 'I know what you mean. Shall we use these ones?' I asked, pulling out some teacups and small plates. After arranging them on a tray, I returned to our conversation. 'Now that you've come this far, you should trust your own sense of what sparks joy. You just said you found lots that didn't. That's your own inner voice speaking. If there are similar shots from different angles, just pick the one you like best.'

'You're right. I know that, but when I actually hold them and try to decide, I start to waver.'

The kettle whistled shrilly, interrupting her. She turned off the gas and poured the boiling water over the tea leaves. I inhaled the calming fragrance of green tea.

'I can relate,' I said. 'But not all photos are destined to be looked at our whole life long. Just like our connections with people. Not everyone we meet will become our close friend or life partner.'

'That's true.' Chiyo lifted the lid of a wooden box on the table, took out some plump round *daifuku* and placed them on the plates.

Hako, who loved *daifuku* with their sweet adzuki bean paste filling and soft mochi wrapper, shook with excitement. 'Yum!' he shouted, but I hastily clamped his lid shut, knowing he couldn't resist anything with bean paste.

'Stop being so greedy,' I said.

'The point is whether you want to recall a certain

memory repeatedly for the rest of your life,' I said. 'So choose the photos you want to keep based on whether they convey memories that will inspire you to live each day positively.'

As if mulling over these words, Chiyo gazed at a bunch of family photos stuck to the fridge door with magnets. Shunsuke and Ikumi at birth. Kindergarten excursions. Elementary school entrance ceremonies. Sports events.

Hako, who'd been struggling against my hand, suddenly stopped and peered at the photos. *Hey! Where's her husband?* he whispered. Chiyo's husband seemed to have disappeared from the photos around the time the children entered junior high.

'My husband got sick when the kids graduated from elementary school,' Chiyo murmured. 'He never got better and, in the end, he died.' After that, she told me, she'd worked as an insurance salesperson, raising their two children on her own.

'So that's what happened,' I said.

'I was always busy and got mad at them a lot. I had very little time to play with them. That's probably why they turned out so cynical.'

'Don't be so hard on yourself, Chiyo.'

Storytelling Photo Albums

'Sorry to go on like that, Miko,' she said. 'Could you tell Shunsuke and Ikumi that the tea's ready?'

I nodded wordlessly and returned to the room with the albums to find Shunsuke and Ikumi staring at some photos spread out on the floor.

'Mum was so busy after Dad died, I thought she never had time to play with us ...' Shunsuke was saying.

'But actually, she did a lot with us, didn't she?' said Ikumi. 'How could we have forgotten?'

Catching sight of me, Shunsuke said, 'Miko, thanks for helping our mother tidy up. As we were tidying the photos, we remembered how much she loved us.'

In the same way people can forget things and memories, parents and children can forget their love for each other. Tidying up can return these precious gifts to us in unexpected ways.

'I'm sorry we were so rude earlier,' said Ikumi. 'We've decided to make an album for our mother of photos that spark joy.'

I beamed at them. 'I'm sure Chiyo will treasure it,' I said gaily.

As long as you guys finally get it, that's just fine, Hako said loftily, nodding sagely in my hands.

We joined Chiyo in the dining room for a short tea break. Sitting around the table, we sipped tea and munched on *daifuku*. I've heard that adzuki beans were once used to ward off evil spirits. Sometimes during a tidying project, I get a heavy feeling, as though I'm dragging the spirits of everything in the home along with me, so sweets like *daifuku* that are made from adzuki beans are a particularly welcome treat.

My adzuki bean-loving buddy was so noisy, I stuck him under the table and let him eat half my *daifuku*. He extended his pink tongue, wrapped it around the *daifuku* and popped it in his mouth. *That's more like it!* he exclaimed, his good mood restored.

As the final step in Chiyo's tidying festival, we began sorting the photos that had been stored in cardboard boxes. There were photos of Shunsuke and Ikumi's high school entrance and graduation ceremonies, as well as photos of them when they were in university, started working and got married. The number of photos from these years dwindled, reflecting that the family had fewer opportunities to take photos together. But then the number shot up again – with the birth of Ikumi's daughter, Ayaka.

Chiyo told us she was so thrilled by her first grandchild she followed her everywhere taking photos with a newly purchased digital camera. 'Ikumi, look!' she suddenly exclaimed. She held up a photo of Ayaka and herself at the same age side by side. 'Doesn't Ayaka look just like me?'

'You're right! Your faces look identical! Even the pose with one hand on the hip is the same!' Ikumi burst out laughing.

'Look at these two pics, you guys,' Shunsuke chimed in. 'Mum and Ayaka. They could be twins. Both doing origami and both smiling in the exact same way. Like they say: blood will tell.'

'I can't believe I looked like cute little Ayaka,' Chiyo said. 'I hated my looks, but now I think I can finally get over that.' She smiled happily.

Tidying up means getting to know yourself. It's a process of discovering your own wonderful qualities. I often meet people who can't put down their phones and are obsessed with social media. They're constantly worrying about how others see them. I encourage these people to tidy up their living space. When we tidy, the things we own will show us the complexes we can do without and the personal characteristics and qualities we should value.

'I feel so much better,' Chiyo told me as she compared the photo of herself as a little girl with that of her granddaughter. 'I'm going to let go of all the ones I wasn't sure of and spend the rest of my life only with those that really bring me joy. Photos of me with Shunsuke and Ikumi, photos of Ayaka, and …' She reached out and picked up a single photo. It was old and faded, taken with film rather than with a digital camera. It was a shot of a much younger Chiyo standing with her husband in front of their newly built house with its aquamarine roof. The picture was out of focus and lopsided, but she and her husband were grinning broadly, and their love for each other was evident.

'That's a great photo, isn't it? You both look so happy.' Ikumi wrapped an arm around Chiyo's shoulders as she gazed at the photo.

'When I married your dad, I wasn't sure if I liked him or not. It was an arranged marriage, and he didn't talk much. But when we were looking through the photos

today, I realised that over the years, while we were raising you, my love for him grew. Even after he died, I've kept on loving him.'

'Mum ...' Tears had welled up in Ikumi's eyes. For some reason, Hako had started sniffling, too.

'But it's so like him, isn't it?' Shunsuke said, wiping his eyes. 'For such an important picture to be out of focus.'

'Yes, that's what I like about it,' said Chiyo. 'It's just like life. Life is blurred and lopsided. Sometimes it's too bright, sometimes too dark. You can't erase it or edit it, unlike photos taken with a digital camera. But some of those moments are treasures.' Chiyo hugged her husband's photo to her chest.

'Do you still have it? Dad's camera? Let's take a photo together,' Shunsuke said.

'I was hoping you'd say that. I already bought a roll of film and got the camera ready.'

Chiyo winked at me. She'd found the camera on our third day of tidying, and she'd begun planning for today from that very moment.

Chiyo, Shunsuke and Ikumi stood together in front of the entrance to their house, lined up in exactly the same spot Chiyo and her husband had stood before. I aimed the camera. And panicked. 'Oh dear. What if mine's out of focus too?'

You're going to be in big trouble, Miko, Hako said, ramping up the pressure.

'I don't care if it's blurred or lopsided,' said Chiyo with a smile.

'Me neither!' Shunsuke and Ikumi said in unison, grinning broadly.

You'll do just fine, came the quiet voice of the camera.

Fortified by these words, I made up my mind, closed my eyes and pressed the shutter.

Chiyo died half a year later. She was already sick and aware of how little time she had left when she asked me to help her complete the final tidying up of her life. She decided to spend her last days with the things she loved and with her beloved family.

The photo used at her funeral was the one I'd taken of the three of them standing outside the house. Just as I'd feared, it was out of focus and on an angle. Although I was mortified by my lack of skill as a photographer,

Ikumi insisted it was a great photo. Chiyo, garbed in royal blue, her face lit up by a beautiful smile.

The following month, Shunsuke and Ikumi treated me to breakfast. They wanted to meet me before I went to work and came all the way, in the rain, to a coffee shop near my house.

After thanking me, Ikumi said, 'We had so much fun tidying up the photos with our mother that day. We hadn't talked together like that as a family for a very long time.'

She was right. That day, the chatty ones hadn't been the photos but rather the family of three sharing their memories. Perhaps the photos had been waiting for someone to come and speak about them.

When we discover something that brings us joy, a conversation is born from the memories it inspires. Things that spark joy have the power to make people talk about those items. And that becomes a family's story.

'If we hadn't tidied up together at the end, we might never have had a heart-to-heart conversation like that before she died,' said Shunsuke. 'We can't thank you enough.' He handed me a photo. It was of me, taken from behind as I walked away from the house with the aquamarine roof down the hill towards the sea. Under my arm was Hako.

'Mum took this shot. It looked like you were talking to that box as you walked down the hill, and she found that funny.' Shunsuke smiled.

It hit me that although I see many photos of my clients, I'd never had one of Hako and me.

Not bad. Although of course, it's out of focus, said Hako. But although he said this with his usual sarcasm, he was grinning.

'Don't say things like that,' I whispered, squeezing his lid shut as I left the coffee shop.

It had stopped raining, and a rainbow spanned the sky. A warm spring breeze blew, stirring the hem of my white dress.

'Time to go, Hako! We've got a big job ahead of us today!'

Honestly! You're such a box – I mean slave – driver.

We were going to tidy up a two-family home. It looked like it was going to be a tough one. What kind of chatty rooms were in store for us there, I wondered. Although the thought overwhelmed me a little, my anxiety was swept away by a surge of elation. I retied my red neckerchief tightly, tucked Hako firmly under one arm and set off at a run.

Epilogue

Recently, I tidied up my own space for the first time in a while. Before I had realised it, I'd let myself become surrounded by clothes and books that didn't spark joy. Even though tidying is my job, there are still times when I forget the things that spark joy for me.

At times like that, I tidy my own space. I touch each thing and listen to what it says. My things teach me what is important to me now. They also help me see what I should do next.

After tidying up, I gazed for a long time at Hako where he sat beside me.

Oh no you don't! he protested. *No need to tidy up in here!*

Although he struggled, I opened his mouth (or rather his lid) and took out one box after another. There was a shocking number of smaller boxes packed inside, making me wonder how he managed to fit them all in.

At the very bottom was an old, familiar one, bright pink in colour. It used to contain an American-made doll that I'd loved as a child. When I picked it up, I heard a voice.

Come to the USA!

It seemed to be calling me from a long way away, and somehow I knew I was destined to go. If I crossed the ocean, there would be many more places to tidy. What kind of chatty rooms awaited me there?

MIKO'S TIDYING TIPS
The Five Key Steps to Tidying

STEP 1 Visualise your ideal lifestyle

What inspired you to tidy up? Before you start discarding things, take some time to really think about why you want to tidy. Picture how you want to live in your newly tidied space, visualising it so concretely that it seems real.

STEP 2 Tidy by category

We can't tidy up because we have too much stuff, and we have too much stuff because we lost track of what's already there. It's important to bring everything in the same category out at once so you can grasp the sheer volume. Instead of tidying by place or room, tidy by category.

STEP 3 Choose what sparks joy when you touch it

The secret of tidying is to focus on what to keep, not on what to discard. When choosing, it's essential to actually touch each item. Listen to what your body tells you, then keep those things that spark joy while letting go of the rest. This way, you'll be left with only the possessions that make you happy and a lifestyle that brings you joy.

STEP 4 Tidy in the right order

There is a correct order to tidying. Start with clothes, then proceed to books, papers, *komono* or miscellaneous items, and finally sentimental items. Following this order makes tidying smoother because it gives you a chance to gradually hone your sense of what spark joys for you.

STEP 5 Decide where everything in your home belongs

Once you've finished choosing the things that spark joy, designate a place for each one. If there are any items without a fixed address, the potential to return to clutter increases dramatically. When everything has a place where it belongs, you can keep your home decluttered simply by putting each thing away after using it.

WORDS TO KEEP IN MIND

Tidying is a Festival

You'll never finish tidying by doing a little every day. Tidying should be treated like a festival and tackled all in one go. Of course, we still need to put things back in their proper place daily, but a tidying festival is something we commit to doing once in our life and finish as quickly as possible. Approach it as a major project that will transform your life, not as an extension of the day-to-day task of putting things away. Tidying is the sacred act of finding a home for all the things that support your life.

Sense of Joy

Focus on what to keep, not on what to throw away. The criterion for choosing is whether an item sparks joy when you touch it. It's important to actually touch or hold each item when you make that decision. When you do, ask yourself if you feel a flutter of joy, or if your body responds in any way. Look at each thing carefully and decide what to keep. As you repeat this process, you'll come to know as soon as you touch something if it sparks joy.

The Purpose of Things

When you come across something you can't bring yourself to throw away even though it doesn't spark joy, think about what its real purpose in your life is. You might realise, for example, that a garment which delighted you when you first bought it doesn't suit

The Five Key Steps to Tidying

you, or that it has lost its thrill over time. In these cases, you can thank that garment for bringing you joy when you bought it and for teaching you what you don't look good in, and then let it go. By teaching you what brings you joy, it has already fulfilled its purpose.

Rebound

'If you try to clean up all at once you'll just return to clutter. You should clean up a little each day to avoid clutter rebound.' This commonly accepted view of tidying is false. By tidying up properly in one shot, you can avoid rebound and keep your space tidy. The correct way to tidy is to keep only things that spark joy and designate each one a place. Doing just this, and doing it all in one go, allows you to see dramatic results. And this causes such a drastic change in your mindset that you'll never return to clutter.

Take Everything Out

When tidying by category, the first step is to gather every single item in the same category from every corner of your home and lay it out in one spot on the floor or a bed. By doing so, you can grasp the total volume of what you have. The shock of seeing how much is there, and the realisation that you have multiple things that are the same, will spur you on to tidy more efficiently and effectively. Besides, when things are put away, you can't tell if they spark joy or not.

Stand Everything Upright

Whether documents, books or clothes, store everything upright. Even stationery utensils, such as stapler refills and erasers in your desk drawer. Fold your clothes, then line them upright inside your chest of drawers or clothes case. Piling clothes on top of each other creates the illusion of unlimited storage space, and we end up with far more clothes than we want. The things on the bottom of the pile are not only harder to get at but easily forgotten, which means their joy factor fades more quickly. By storing things upright in a restricted space, you can tell at a glance when the volume is expanding.

Rising to the Right

Hang clothes in the closet so they rise to the right. Lines with an upward curve lift our spirits; this principle applies in the closet, too. As a rule of thumb, hang clothes in the same category together, such as coats, jackets and shirts. Like people, clothes feel more comfortable when they are with things of the same type. For the same reason, don't jam them in too tightly. By following these simple rules, you'll get a rush of joy each time you open your closet.

Tapping into the Art of Origami

I think Japanese people come equipped with 'folding genes'. Although Japan is well known for its beautiful origami, paper is not the only thing the Japanese fold. Notably, their traditional clothing – kimono and yukata – are folded into smooth, neat rectangles so they can be stored in drawers. We should fold everything that can be folded with the same approach as origami. No matter what the shape of a piece of clothing, fold it so that it becomes a compact rectangle. Use your whole hand, not just the tips of your fingers, and stroke the cloth with your palm. The warmth of your hand will smooth out wrinkles and breathe life into the fabric.

Cut the Umbilical Cords

Products displayed in a store seem reserved and aloof. It's only when they're brought home and the tags are removed that they feel like they belong. When tags are left on newly purchased products, the energy of the things already in the home can so overwhelm them that they fade into the background. They'll be shoved off into a corner and, in the end, forgotten. So be sure to remove the tags as soon as you buy something. This will cut the umbilical cord that joins them to the store and make them feel welcome in your home.

Different Shades of Siblings

For some reason, when people have two garments of different colours in a design they really like, one garment tends to get far more wear than the other, which usually remains put away. I often hear such 'siblings' fighting when I open a client's closet. Odder still, even when people buy two items of identical design and colour, one of them gets worn while the other doesn't, resulting in jealous bickering. It's time to say goodbye to one of the siblings.

Wake Up Your Books

Don't skip the step of removing all your books from the shelves. Books left too long in a bookcase fall asleep. It's hard to tell just by gazing at sleeping books whether or not they spark joy. We first need to wake them up by moving them, letting the air in and giving them some stimulation. Books that have been piled up can be woken by slapping their covers. A big mound of books can be roused by clapping your hands in front of it, just like

Japanese people do at a Shinto shrine to draw the god's attention. Waking up our books also wakens the senses, sharpening our ability to recognise what sparks joy.

Books that Lose Their Flavour and Books Whose Flavour Deepens

Some books lose their flavour. You may have begged someone to give you a book and read it avidly the first time, but now it doesn't spark anything at all. Or you may have read the book many times, absorbing all it had to give until it lost its richness and flavour. That's a sign it's time to let the book go. Conversely, there are books that, no matter how often you read them, are still fascinating and whose flavour seems to deepen over time, like dried squid when chewed. Tidying up our bookshelves is the process of being reunited with words we love and discovering memories associated with books.

Bloated Kitchens

A set of cups received as a gift that's still in its box, a cocktail shaker you thought you might use someday, a large stock of canned food, leftover jam jars. Things like these indicate your kitchen has gained too much stuff and is suffering from bloating. Particularly after disasters, the number of people who hoard emergency goods and food supplies tends to increase. To manage your food stock properly, first bring every item out of storage and count what you have. Decide the volume of each necessity you would realistically need in a disaster, as well as in daily life, for the span of a week or a month, and keep your stock within that amount so that your storage space isn't filled to excess.

A Beautiful Rainbow

The trick to tidying is to store things with similar functions or characteristics near each other, such as storing food containers like empty jars and Tupperware together or chopstick holders in the same place as chopsticks. *Komono* or miscellaneous items, which are harder to categorise, can also be stored this way, such as by putting computer-related items with electrical cords because they 'smell' of electricity. By playing this kind of word association game in your mind, you can come up with an arrangement in which your storage is a gradation from one thing to the next. Storage is the task of harmonising diverse elements to make a beautiful rainbow in your home.

Noisy Labels

Take a look around your home. Do you see any stickers or packaging on things like your clothes cases or air freshener? A room may look well tidied at first glance, but slogans like 'Extra Storage' or 'Refreshens Instantly!' assert their presence. This is why even people who have kept their possessions reduced and are good at storage end up being one step away from perfectly tidy. Words within our line of vision fill a space with endless and unsettling chatter. For this reason, remove any labels and stickers on products as soon as you buy them. This one small act can greatly increase your peace of mind

The Sun Strategy

If you wish that the people you live with would tidy up too, take a hint from 'The North Wind and the Sun'. This fable by Aesop teaches us that encouraging people in a natural way is far more effective than trying to force them to take action. Likewise with tidying, it's more effective to say nothing and focus on putting your own space in order than to nag or lecture others. Inspired by your actions, the people who live with you will start tidying of their own accord. Tidying causes a chain reaction, so if you feel frustrated by other people's things, try using the Sun Strategy.

Tidying Is Like a Mini-Move

Moving is not just a chance to relocate to a new place but also an excellent opportunity to find the lifestyle that suits you. A tidying festival means selecting only the things you need for your new life. That's what makes it like a mini-move. By parting with things like accessories you've never used, old love letters from someone you've left behind, or  clothes your mother picked for you, you can reach for a happiness that is yours, one where you live surrounded only by the things you love. Tidying has the power to dramatically change your life.

Remember to Say Thank You

It's important to feel gratitude towards your things. When you change your clothes, when you remove your accessories, when you return your handbag to your closet, thank them. If we are grateful for the things that support our lives on a daily basis, they will become our allies. We should also thank them when it's time to let them go, saying, 'Thank you for the joy you brought me when I bought you,' and, 'Thank you for standing by me all this time.' To 'discard' something is not to treat it with disrespect, but rather to set it free with gratitude.

The stories presented here were originally published as a series in *Yomiuri Shimbun* from October 2020 to April 2021 and were revised and supplemented for publication as a book.

Miko's Tidying Tips is a revised version of an article published in the April 2022 edition of the magazine *Casa Brutus*.